TILLY'S PONY TAILS

Red Admiral

the racehorse

TILLY'S PONY TAILS

Red Admiral
the racehorse

PIPPA FUNNELL

Illustrated by Jennifer Miles

Orion
Children's Books

First published in Great Britain in 2009
by Orion Children's Books
a division of the Orion Publishing Group Ltd
Orion House
5 Upper St Martin's Lane
London WC2H 9EA
An Hachette UK Company

5 7 9 8 6 4

A catalogue record for this book is available from the British Library.

ISBN 978 1 84255 710 5

Printed and bound by CPI Group (UK) Ltd, Croydon, CR0 4YY

www.orionbooks.co.uk

For my mother,
Jenny Nolan

One

Tilly Redbrow was mad about horses. Her favourite way to spend time was at Silver Shoe Farm. In fact, it was like a second home to her. Ever since Tilly helped rescue a mysterious horse called Magic Spirit, she had been a regular visitor.

As often as she could, Tilly would be there, helping Angela, who ran the stables. Over the months, Tilly learned how to groom and muck out. She'd made new friends called Cally and Mia, and helped them to care for Rosie – the pretty strawberry roan pony they shared. But what Tilly liked most of all, was spending time with Magic Spirit. She had a special friendship with him. Tilly was the person Magic Spirit trusted most, and although he'd been underweight and unhappy when he'd arrived at the stables, he was growing stronger and healthier by the week. One day he was going to be a fabulous horse.

Tilly loved helping to care for the horses, but what she was really looking forward to was learning how to ride. Every time she saw people getting ready in the yard, saddling up and heading out on some of the forest hacks, or going to the indoor school for lessons, she longed to be doing the same.

The chance of a ride was all she could think about as she sat down for breakfast, twiddling the horsehair bracelet she'd worn all her life. It was Saturday, so the whole family were at the table, chatting and taking their time.

"Good morning, dreamy," said Tilly's mum, passing her the cereal. Tilly always chose muesli with chopped banana, followed by a big glass of orange juice.

Mr Redbrow looked up from his newspaper and smiled.

"Morning, Tiger Lil'. The weather's going to be lovely today. What about a fishing trip to the river with me and Adam?" he asked, with a wink.

Adam was Tilly's younger brother. He was busy flicking bits of toast across the table. He was annoying in the way that little brothers sometimes can be.

All Tilly wanted to do was spend the day with the horses. It was the first hot day in May, and she knew the stable yard was going to be buzzing with activity. Adam just grinned at her and poked out his tongue.

"But I guess you'll be going to Silver Shoe Farm," her dad continued, as if he was reading her mind. "Adam and I will have to go fishing on our own. You know, some parents complain that their children sit around doing nothing at the weekend! Not you though, eh, Tilly? You're always doing something – as long as it involves horses!"

Tilly caught her dad's eye. Despite what he said, she knew that really he was happy for her, and proud of her hard work. He understood what horses meant to her.

"Oh, look," said Tilly's mum, studying the date at the top of the newspaper. "It's nearly the end of the month. Not long till your birthday, Tilly. Perhaps you'll want a sleepover? Have you thought about what you want for a present yet?"

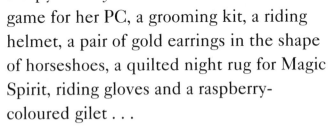

Tilly had a huge list in her mind: another year's subscription to *Pony* magazine, a pair of canary yellow jodhpurs, a copy of *Pony Ranch!* game for her PC, a grooming kit, a riding helmet, a pair of gold earrings in the shape of horseshoes, a quilted night rug for Magic Spirit, riding gloves and a raspberry-coloured gilet . . .

She shut her eyes and reeled off the list. Then she decided to go for the big one.

"Riding lessons – at the farm. It would be extra great if you could get me those!"

"Hmm, we'll have to see about that," said her mum, exchanging glances with Mr Redbrow.

Underneath the table, Tilly had her fingers crossed.

Just then, her phone buzzed. She pulled it out of her pocket and checked the message. She knew straightaway that it would be from either Mia or Cally.

PERFECT DAY. IF U R NOT AT THE FARM BY 10AM
THEN U R A LOSER! LOVE MIA XXX

Tilly laughed.

"Dad," she said, as she swallowed a mouthful of muesli. "If you're taking Adam fishing soon, then can you give me a lift to Silver Shoe Farm on your way?"

"Whatever you say, Tiger Lil'."

"Thanks, Dad!"

12

Two

They drove along the now familiar leafy lane that led to Silver Shoe Farm. Eventually they pulled up at the five-bar gate and Tilly said goodbye to her dad and Adam. She marched across the yard, straight to Magic Spirit's large stable, which was more like a barn, situated at the back of the yard. Sure enough, there he was, happily munching some hay.

"Hello, boy!" she said. She couldn't believe how well he was looking. He had

put on weight, his coat was getting its shine back and most of the sores had gone. Tilly remembered going into his stable for the first time. Back then his coat had been matted and filthy. His eyes had been wild and his whole body tense. He had startled and nearly knocked her over. Today, he was peaceful and relaxed. It was almost as though he was a different horse.

Magic Spirit looked up at Tilly and immediately came towards her. His ears pricked forward at the sound of her voice.

"You do look handsome," she said, stroking his neck proudly. Magic Spirit nuzzled her shoulder.

Duncan, Angela's head boy, appeared in the doorway with some mucking out tools.

"Hello, guys. I thought I'd find you in here, Tilly. I saw your dad drop you off. Just in time . . ."

Tilly saw that he was holding a shovel and bucket.

"Do you think you'd be able to muck out Magic Spirit's stable and then give him a brush down?"

"Sure," said Tilly eagerly.

"You can tie him up outside."

"Where's his head collar?" asked Tilly, noticing that Magic Spirit wasn't wearing one.

"I've got a smart new leather one," said Duncan, handing it to Tilly. "Do you want to see if it fits?"

Tilly approached Magic, chatting away and telling him what she was about to do, as if he understood her every word. She knew he didn't like sudden movements around his head, so she reassured him by rubbing his favourite spot at the base of his wither.

Before putting the head collar on him, she undid the clip attached to the strap under the throat, and let the headpiece out onto the last hole so it would be easier to get on. Then she slipped the noseband over Magic's nose and quietly pulled the headpiece over his ears. Once it was in place, she clipped the throat strap back and adjusted the buckle, so it was two holes tighter, but not too tight. She had seen from pictures that head collars were fitted more loosely than bridles.

Magic Spirit stood very still, and even helped a little by lowering his head.

"That's it," said Duncan, watching her. "Gently swing the head strap behind Magic's ears, but be careful not to drag it over his eyes, ears, or nose."

Duncan clipped the lead rope to the ring on the underside of the halter and offered it to Tilly. Her stomach filled with butterflies. She reached for the rope, but she was so excited and overwhelmed by the thought of actually leading Magic Spirit by herself, she could hardly move. She just stared at him adoringly.

"Go for it," urged Duncan.

He showed her how to hold the rope, avoiding looping it around her own hand.

"If the rope is looped around your hand you risk getting rope burns if he pulls away," he explained. "Now, stand at his shoulder and give him his cue. I usually give one click and then say 'walk on' which he seems to respond to. Although he doesn't seem to have been broken in yet, he's obviously had some experience of being led in the past."

"How old do you think he is?" asked Tilly.

"He's a four year old – still young." Duncan had looked at Magic's teeth once he'd become calm enough to handle. "That's how you judge a horse's age," he explained.

Tilly positioned herself at Magic Spirit's shoulder, and smiled at him. He gave her a little nod, as if to say, 'I'm ready'. In her

head she counted to three then clicked
once and spoke out loud:

"Walk on, boy."

It was clear that Magic Spirit
understood. He walked forward without
any further prompting.

"That's perfect," said Duncan, behind
them. "You've got such a good way with
horses, Tilly."

As they walked together into the sunlight, Tilly beamed with pride. The smell of honeysuckle and freshly-mown grass drifted towards them.

Even though it was only a short distance to the tie-up ring on the far wall, Tilly's confidence grew with every step and it felt as though they'd covered a large amount of ground.

"Whoa, boy!"

Together Magic Spirit and Tilly stood still, and Duncan caught up with them.

"Great. Now, allow a length of rope so that he's free to move and look around, not too long . . . and then I'll show you how to tie him safely."

Duncan took the rope from Tilly and demonstrated a quick release knot. Tilly watched closely, but she was still a bit confused.

"Don't worry," laughed Duncan, seeing the expression on her face. "It takes practice. If you join the Pony Club and get some riding lessons you'll learn all the skills you need. But if you're not sure about something, you can always ask. It's better to ask than take a risk."

Tilly wondered what the chance of getting lessons would be. Maybe for her birthday? She hoped her mum and dad would agree that it was a good idea – she'd do anything. Everybody's chores for a week, a hundred hours of homework . . . she'd even sell some of her old My Little Pony toy collection (which she had started when she was five) – it didn't seem quite so cool, now that she had the real thing standing next to her!

Three

After mucking out the stable and grooming
Magic Spirit, Tilly met up with her friends,
Cally and Mia. They'd finished grooming
Rosie and were in the club room, making
lemonade.

"Real lemons and loads of sugar," said
Mia, as she poured the ingredients into a
jug.

"It's the yummiest thing," added Cally.
"We always make it whenever there's a
sunny weekend. It gives us energy.

We're going to have a canter this afternoon
– there's a really nice wide route around the
edge of the fields and it's dried up enough
now after the wet spring. I'm taking Rosie,
and Mia's riding a dapple grey Connemara
called Bunny."

"Bunny belongs to Zoe Lampeter,"
explained Mia. "She's another girl at the
stables, but she's staying with her mum in
America so she hasn't been able to ride for
weeks. Zoe's mum asked if we'd exercise
Bunny until she gets back."

"You're so lucky," said Tilly. "I wish
I could go riding with you this afternoon."

"Why don't you ask Angela if you can?" said Cally excitedly. "She might let you come if one of us leads you."

"Let's down our lemonade and then go and ask her!"

Angela was just about to go into the sand school with one of her horses. Cally asked whether there was a chance that Tilly might go out with her and Mia, but Angela shook her head.

"I'm sorry, Tilly, but all the ponies and horses are out – the ones that would be safe for you to ride anyway. And I think you should have some lessons in the school first. It's just not possible today."

Tilly couldn't hide her disappointment. She stared at the ground and played with one of her plaits. Cally and Mia looked disappointed too.

"I tell you what," said Angela encouragingly. "If you can get here tomorrow afternoon, about two o'clock, we could sort something out for then. I've had a cancellation of a private lesson, so I could spend the time with you and go over the basics. Call it my way of thanking you for all your hard work with Magic Spirit. Would that be okay?"

Tilly's disappointment turned into happiness. She could barely speak to say thank you. She nodded her head and grinned. Cally and Mia gave her a hug, and together the three of them jumped up and down with excitement.

"Wow! A private lesson with Angela," whispered Mia. "And you said you thought we were lucky! She knows everything there is to know about riding!"

"I'd better get started," called Angela. "And you girls should go and get tacked up if you want to make the most of the good weather. What about you, Tilly? As you're not riding, maybe you could go and see how my dad's getting on with Red Admiral. He came from Ben Hedges' yard – he's a well-known trainer of National Hunt horses, you know, horses who jump steeplechase fences and hurdles. You'll find them in the wash box, where Dad is endlessly hosing Red Admiral's leg. He got a tendon injury at his very first race meeting. He stumbled as he landed after one of the hurdles and one of his hind legs struck into his front causing a very serious injury. The vet reckons it's unlikely he'll ever race again. The owners sent him to us

25

eight months ago, as a last resort, to see if we can get him right . . . maybe he needs some of your special magic, Tilly."

Cally and Mia disappeared into the tack room, and Tilly headed for the washbox in the main yard. She could find her way round the stables easily now, because every night she lay awake thinking about it. Every little corner of the yard was clear in her mind.

She could see Jack Fisher with Red Admiral. Red was the most magnificent looking thoroughbred, a very red chestnut with a copper gleam to his coat and a white blaze on his nose.

Even standing in the washbox, Tilly thought he had a regal manner, a look that said 'I'm going to be king of the race course'.

Jack was busy hosing Red's injured leg, and talking to the vet. It was clear from the leg's size, below the knee down to the fetlock, that it was more filled than the other one. Jack sighed. He'd spent five months walking Red in hand, hosing his leg twice a day. Over the last three months, his work had been stepped up, putting Duncan in the saddle. Yesterday Red had had his

first piece of fast work, but today it didn't look good. His leg had filled again and looked swollen, and he was walking shorter, not wanting to put weight on it.

Four

The vet was a tall man called Brian. He
and Jack Fisher were obviously old friends.
They chatted and joked about all sorts of
things, mainly to do with horse racing.
Tilly climbed onto a bale of hay and sat
down. The men didn't notice her, as she
watched and listened to their conversation.

She learned that Jack was working with
four young thoroughbreds at the stables,
including Red Admiral. Each of them was
actually owned by someone different. He

was responsible for rehabilitating and looking after them. Tilly couldn't believe it when she heard how much money the horses were worth. Red Admiral, in particular, had been valued at £100,000 before his accident.

That was more money than she could possibly imagine. She nearly gasped out loud.

"He's one of the best we've had," said Jack. "Great breeding – his sire was a former champion. The Brigdales have high hopes for him."

Tilly assumed the Brigdales must be Red Admiral's owners.

"He's cost them a small fortune. They're

shattered about the news he may not race again, so I'll do everything I can to get him back. If he comes back, he's sure to make them some big money . . ."

Brian raised his eyebrows.

"Impressive," he said.

"Absolutely," agreed Jack, scratching his belly. "Trouble is, that tendon is still not a hundred percent. End of June, we wanted to run him at the Cosford race meeting."

"Well, as I said," explained the vet. "I've got no concerns. I've checked him over and the ultrasound scan suggests the tendon will be fine. I think the swelling is from stretching the scar tissue, having galloped for all that time. Keep hosing and icing it. I guess it's up to him now."

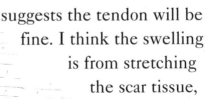

31

"If he doesn't get it together, The Brigdales are going to be disappointed. All that money they've invested . . ."

"It's not just money that's at stake though, is it, Jack?" said Brian. "It's all your time and hard work."

Jack let out a long breath.

"The Brigdales told me if I can get Red Admiral sound and fit, I can keep him and train him here. They won't send him back to Ben Hedges' place. But if I can't get him fit enough to race, he'll be retired and given to Cavendish Hall as a school horse. He has such a wonderful temperament, but it would be a tragic waste."

Tilly realised that perhaps she wasn't meant to hear this part of the conversation. She slipped down from the hay bale and sneaked into the yard. It was quiet outside, because everyone had gone hacking. A broom was resting against the wall, so she picked it up and began sweeping.

As she swept, she thought about what she had overheard. She felt bad for Jack –

she knew Silver Shoe deserved to have a special horse like Red Admiral, and she knew that Jack had always dreamed of training a winner. He wouldn't take a risk with a horse that wasn't ready. Then she remembered what Angela had said to her: 'some of your special magic might help'. What did she mean by that? Tilly leaned against the broom handle and twiddled with her horsehair bracelet. Perhaps she needed to spend some quiet time with Red Admiral.

Eventually, Jack and the vet went over to the club room. When they had gone, Tilly went back into the stables. She unbolted the door and crept inside. It took a while for her eyes to adjust to the sudden darkness, and for a moment, she couldn't see anything. She found Red Admiral in his stable looking sorry for himself.

"Oh, Red Admiral. You poor thing," she whispered gently. "I hear you've hurt your leg. Let me have a look."

At first, Red Admiral didn't respond, but when she held out her arm, she noticed his ears prick up. He walked towards her and as soon as he was close enough, started sniffing at her horsehair bracelet.

"How strange!" exclaimed Tilly. "That's exactly what Magic Spirit likes to do."

He worked his nose around the bracelet and then along her arm, until he was practically licking her face. Tilly laughed and stroked his forehead.

"That's more like it," she smiled. "So you like my bracelet, eh? Well, maybe I'll make one out of your hairs. You have such a beautiful tail. Jack Fisher is going to make you a champion one day, you'll see."

Red Admiral lifted his head and stood tall and proud, in the narrow shaft of sunlight. Then he started to nuzzle the horsehair bracelet again, almost chewing it off her wrist.

"Let me see your leg," Tilly whispered.

She leaned down beside his injured foreleg which was bandaged. She took the bandage off and instinctively she ran her hand down the back of his tendon. Gradually, with her fingers, she began to massage the area from the knee down to

the fetlock. As she did, Red Admiral
lowered his head and stood still.

Suddenly Tilly had that strange feeling
again, the same one she'd had with Magic
Spirit, as if everything else had disappeared
and only she and Red Admiral existed.
They were lost in the moment and only
aware of each other. So much so, that neither
of them noticed when Duncan walked in
and stood for a second, watching them.

Eventually Tilly re-bandaged the leg
and stood up. She patted Red Admiral on
the shoulder and then, careful not to get
behind him in case he decided to kick, she
ran her fingers through his tail. She
gathered up the loose hairs and put them in
her pocket, so that later she could weave
them into a bracelet.

"You'll be fine, Red. I know you will,"
she said, patting him one more time before
leaving the stable. "I'll see you again
soon."

Five

When Tilly got home, she spent two hours on the internet, looking up riding tips, so that she would know exactly what to do during her lesson next day. Her dad agreed to take her to the farm for two o'clock, as long she helped make supper. Tilly's mum had gone out with friends and wouldn't be back till late, but she had left instructions for cooking spaghetti bolognaise, which was always a popular choice in the Redbrow household.

Tilly was sitting at the computer, with Scruff, the family's long-haired Jack Russell, lying at her feet, chewing on his favourite squeaky toy, when her dad called up to her.

"Tiger Lil'! It's time to make dinner. You promised you'd help!"

But Tilly had just found a brilliant pony-lovers' chat room, where she could

post questions and get advice from other riders. She wasn't ready to finish.

"Five more minutes, Dad – please!"

She could hear her dad muttering something in the kitchen, followed by the sound of pots and pans being clanked about. He wasn't the best of cooks, which is probably why he'd asked for her help.

Fifteen minutes later, Tilly was still at the computer. She had lost track of time, typing responses to a chat room member called 'MyPonyRocks'. It was nice to be able to answer questions as well as ask them. She knew exactly what to say when MyPonyRocks typed:

Can u help?? I adore my twelve-year-old chestnut, but for some reason she gets ultra-nervous around other horses at her stables.

She's especially scared of the big ones. How can I make her more confident around other horses?

Tilly thought of how Duncan had helped Magic Spirit to gain more confidence around the other ponies and horses, by introducing him to a friendly miniature pony called Thumbalina. She quickly typed a reply:

Try introducing her to another friendly pony that is smaller than her, maybe a miniature or Shetland, to help build her confidence. We did this with my favourite horse, Magic Spirit. He was scared of other horses too. Now, he's much happier and really likes his new friend. Good luck. Tilly. x

By the time Tilly got to the kitchen, the spaghetti bolognaise was ready, but there was mess everywhere. Mr Redbrow wasn't impressed.

"You took so long, Tiger Lil', I had to get Adam to help me."

Tilly glanced at Adam, who was standing at the sink, licking tomato sauce from his fingers. It was all over his face, and the worktop, and the floor, and the oven.

"You didn't help with the cooking," he grinned. "So you've got to tidy up!"

41

That night, Tilly dreamed she was watching Red Admiral win his first race and everyone was standing at the winning post cheering him on. The jockey looked up and waved at Tilly, as they crossed the finishing line one length in front of the second horse. Oddly, the jockey appeared to be Tilly's best friend, Becky, who had no interest in horses and often told Tilly she was pony crazy.

It was morning before she knew it. Tilly woke up and yawned. She washed her face and went downstairs to the kitchen.

"Morning, Tilly. Did you sleep well? It was so stuffy in the night, I kept waking up . . . Why is there tomato sauce all over the fridge door?" said her mum, with a puzzled expression.

Tilly winced and said nothing.

"Looks like there's going to be a thunderstorm today – that should clear the air. Although I hope the rain doesn't spoil your shopping trip with Becky."

At first, Tilly didn't take in what her mum had said. She poured some orange juice into a glass and started thinking about whether the thunderstorm would affect her riding lesson with Angela. She hoped not.

"Dad's taking me to Silver Shoe at two o'clock today," she beamed. "Angela's going to give me my first riding lesson, to say thank you for all my hard work at the stables."

Mrs Redbrow put the coffee pot down on the table.

"Oh dear, Tilly. You must have forgotten . . ."

"Forgotten what?"

"Your shopping trip – to North Cosford – with Becky. You girls planned it weeks ago. You were so excited when I agreed to let you go to town on your own together."

With that, Tilly remembered. An awful sick feeling rose in her stomach. She knew how much Becky had been looking forward to their first proper girly shopping trip together – *without* adults. And she'd been looking forward to it too, but all the excitement of Silver Shoe Farm had distracted her.

Tilly's mum frowned.

"You can't let Becky down now. She's your best friend."

"But Angela's offered to give me a private lesson. I can't let *her* down either. This might be my only chance!"

"Oh, I'm sure they'll be other chances, Tilly. Don't you worry."

Tilly knew her mum was right. And she

44

knew it wasn't fair to cancel her plans with Becky at such short notice, but she couldn't help feeling disappointed. The lesson with Angela had made her feel so overwhelmingly happy – the thought of it not happening was crushing. Then she thought of Mia and Cally, going off to ride for the afternoon, or the girls from Cavendish Hall, trotting through the village on their perfect ponies. She felt envious of them all. She couldn't help it.

"It's not fair!" she said, standing up, feeling suddenly tearful and angry. "This is all I've ever wanted and now you're making me miss it to go on a stupid shopping trip with Becky!"

"Tilly!" said her mum, surprised by her daughter's outburst. "This isn't like you! I know how much you want to learn to ride, but it can't be the be all and end all."

"It *is*!" snapped Tilly, as she stormed out of the kitchen.

She found Scruff in the hallway, licking his paws, and before he had a chance to react, she pulled a long coat over her pyjamas, tugged on her trainers, grabbed his lead, clipped it to his collar, and marched out of the house.

Six

Just as Tilly's mum had predicted, the sky
was thundery grey. It looked as if the clouds
would burst any minute now, and soak
everything. Tilly didn't care. She stomped
up the road with a bewildered Scruff
scampering to keep up with her. At first she
didn't think about where she was going, but
somehow she found herself heading for the
road that led to Silver Shoe Farm.

"I'll walk *all* the way there," she hissed
at Scruff, her teethed clenched.

Tilly knew she was only allowed to take Scruff for walks along the roads and pathways near Lower Norbury. Her mum and dad would be worried if they knew she was planning to go so far from the village. But she was too annoyed to think sensibly.

"It's not fair, Scruff! It's not fair!"

Scruff sniffed her ankles.

"Honestly, I didn't mean to say that the shopping trip with Becky was stupid – the words just came out of my mouth. I don't want to be horrible to her. She's my best friend . . . it's just . . ."

Tilly sighed.

"I really, *really* want to learn to ride. You understand don't you, Scruff?"

He looked up and wagged his tail.

The pair of them marched past the sign for Lower Norbury, and started along the narrow pavement of the busy road.

After ten minutes, a loud rumbling noise filled the air – the first clap of thunder. Scruff yapped nervously so Tilly picked him up. Seconds later, the downpour started. Cold, fat raindrops bounced off the leaves and the tarmac.

"Uh, oh!" cried Tilly, cuddling Scruff tightly. "We're gonna get soaked!"

She glanced around, but the only shelter was a bus stop up the road.

"I suppose it's better than nothing," she muttered, and ran through the rain towards it. It didn't help that she was still wearing her pyjamas!

By the time Tilly and Scruff reached the bus stop, they were drenched. Several cars zoomed past them, splashing up puddles of

water. They sat on a wooden bench and waited for the rain to stop. The thought of walking home, wet and cold, wasn't pleasant.

Tilly reached for her phone, thinking that her dad might be able to pick her up, but then she remembered that her phone was still in her jeans' pocket – and she was still in her pyjamas.

"What are we going to do *now*?" she shrugged, feeling silly and pathetic. Scruff put his head on her lap and whimpered.

The sight of the driving rain made Tilly wonder whether the Silver Shoe horses were outside getting wet, or whether they were all cosy in their stables. She knew that Magic Spirit wouldn't like the loud thunderclaps and hoped he wasn't too frightened. And what about poor Becky? Tilly pictured her, sitting at home, staring out of the window and worrying that the rain would spoil the shopping trip she'd been looking forward to for so long. She felt guilty.

Just then, a four-wheel drive pulled into the bus stop. The passenger window came

down. Tilly looked in and saw it was
Angela.

"Goodness me, Tilly!" she said. "What
are you doing out here in the rain? You're
shivering! Hop in. I'll give you a lift."

Relieved, Tilly climbed in. She was
almost too cold to speak. Angela reached
for a spare jacket on the back seat and
wrapped it around her shoulders.

"Who's this?" she said.

"He's called Scruff," Tilly whispered.
"He's our dog."

"He's sweet," said Angela. "Do your
parents know you've come all this way in
the rain? You're nearly at Silver Shoe – your
riding lesson isn't until two o'clock."

With that, Tilly started to cry. She was
so cold and confused she couldn't stop
herself, but Angela was very kind.

"Oh dear, what's happened?"

"I just wanted my first riding lesson,"
sobbed Tilly. "I forgot I was supposed to be
meeting Becky, and now I feel really bad . . .
and I want to do both . . . but there isn't

enough time . . . and no one knows that I came all this way . . . and I haven't got my phone with me . . . and now I'm so cold . . ."

Angela gave her a tissue and rubbed Tilly's shoulder until she was calm again.

"Okay, Tilly. How about this for a good plan? I'll ring your mum and dad and explain where you are, and we'll fix up another day for you to have a riding lesson. It doesn't have to be today – not if you've got other plans."

"But I thought this was my only chance . . . because you had a cancellation . . ."

"Of course not. I want to help you to learn to ride, Tilly. I think you've got a special talent with the horses. Let me talk to your mum and dad about it."

On the way back to the Redbrows' house, Tilly and Angela talked about lots of things, but particularly about riding and friendship and how important it was to have both.

"When I was younger," explained Angela, "I was always going off with my mates and forgetting to do my jobs around the stables. My dad and I argued constantly about it."

Tilly listened.

"Ever since I was a small kid I'd been working with the horses – every morning, every evening and every weekend. It was the family business. But when I was a

teenager, I rebelled. I realised how much I loved the horses in the end, though. My advice to you, Tilly, is to find a balance. You need horses in your life, but you also need your family and friends."

Tilly knew that Angela was talking lots of sense. She sat back and watched the windscreen wipers swish from side to side, and felt warm and happy again.

Seven

Tilly's parents were so relieved to see Tilly safe, they weren't cross with her for walking away from the village. As Angela's four-wheel drive pulled up, they waved from the front door.

"She looks like a drowned rat!" said Adam.

"You silly sausage!" said Tilly's mum, hugging her and kissing the top of her head. It was good to be home.

Mr Redbrow stood in the hallway

talking with Angela. Tilly wanted to hear
what they were saying, but her mum was
fussing so much, she rushed her straight
upstairs for a hot bath.

By the time she came down again, Angela had gone.

"Don't worry," said her dad. "Angela has arranged another lesson for you, next Thursday after school. Although I suppose you'll want more than one, once you get the taste for it."

Tilly nodded, wide-eyed.

"How many lessons will she need?" asked Mrs Redbrow, as she ran a comb through Tilly's wet hair.

"Well, it depends how quickly she learns," explained her dad. "Angela said there are different kinds: group lessons, private tuition. We'll start with one and see how it goes."

Tilly had her fingers crossed again. The more lessons she had, the quicker she would improve, and the closer she'd get to the chance of one day owning her own horse.

After lunch, Tilly received a text from Becky saying:

> HEY T! CAN'T WAIT TO GO SHOPPING. WHAT ARE
> YOU WEARING? X

She knew she'd done the right thing. She quickly sent one back saying:

> SKINNY JEANS AND MY GREEN TOP.
> CAN'T WAIT EITHER! SEE YOU SOON. X

Fortunately the rain had stopped and the sky was blue again. Tilly and her mum drove to Becky's house, picked her up, and then took the short route into North Cosford.

"Have a great time, girls," she said, as Tilly and Becky got out of the car. "I'll meet you back here at four-thirty."

Becky was so excited she tripped over the pavement, which made the pair of them burst into fits of giggles. Tilly's mum smiled and shook her head, then drove away.

"Freedom!" cried Becky, throwing her arms up in the air.

"Hurrah!" grinned Tilly. "Where first?"

"Let's go to Topshop, then Claire's Accessories, and then Debenhams. We can go to the beauty counters and try perfumes on!"

"Good plan – let's get bubble-gum slushies from the newsagent on the way."

"And strawberry laces."

"And maybe after Debenhams we can go to the riding shop on Green Street."

"If we must," groaned Becky. "But only if we can go to HMV after that – I want to look at CDs."

"Agreed."

Together, the girls tumbled into the newsagents and bought their sweets and slushies. Then they headed straight for the undercover shopping precinct.

In Topshop, Becky picked out armfuls of clothes to try on. Most of them were far too big for her, in adult sizes eight, ten and twelve, but she insisted she was hunting for a sophisticated look. She trailed up and down the aisles, with Tilly following.

"If I get through the auditions for *The X Factor*, I'll need to look super-stylish," Becky explained, as she stroked her hand across a gold sequined vest. "Oh, look! I saw this top in Mizz magazine – it's lush!

The girls stumbled into the changing rooms, and started matching things together, creating outfits for Becky to try on. Shiny blue trousers with a white shirt and a chunky belt. Baggy jeans with a cropped sailor jacket and stripy vest. A leopard print ball gown, with a giant bow, and neon green leggings.

"That's the one!" laughed Tilly. "That's the outfit that will get you noticed on *The X Factor*!"

"But I want them to notice my voice more than my outfit," said Becky, examining herself in the mirror. Too late, because

Tilly was distracted – she'd lost interest in the fancy party clothes and was daydreaming about wearing a smart dressage outfit: a top hat and a tail coat.

After visiting Claire's Accessories, where Tilly bought two sets of hair toggles for her plaits – one with lucky horseshoes and another with silver bows – they went to Pony Pride, the riding shop on Green Street.

The moment Tilly stepped inside, her eyes bulged. This was *her* kind of clothes shopping. The racks were full of the latest gear and accessories: denim-look jodhpurs, trendy gilets in pastel colours, quilted jackets and waterproofs, and polo shirts in every colour imaginable.

When she got to the boot section, Tilly was overwhelmed by the choice. There were jodhpur boots, long boots, waterproof

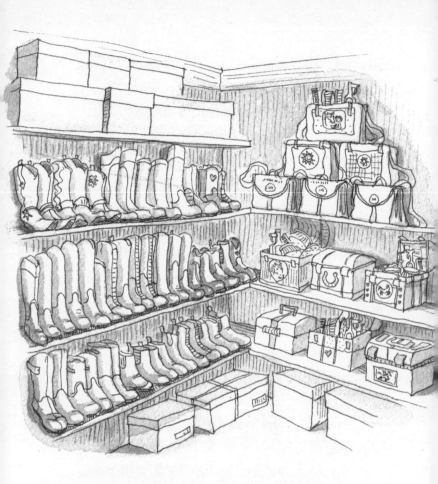

wellington boots, and even a range of
cowboy boots. Her eyes were drawn to a
pair of polished Toggi black zip-up jodhpur
boots. She took one of them off the shelf
and studied it. It smelled of new leather
and felt sturdy and comfortable.

The assistant came over and asked if Tilly needed help.

"That's a great boot," she explained. "Everyone's going for zips these days because it makes them so much easier to get on and off."

"How much are they?" asked Tilly.

"Very reasonable," the shop assistant replied, and told her the price.

Tilly gulped.

"Let's go and look at the grooming kits," she said, nudging Becky, who had found a seat and was looking bored.

To Tilly's relief, the grooming kits were much more affordable. Some of them came in lovely cases or bags, and had everything you would need: dandy brushes, curry combs, body brushes, hoof picks. Some of them came with a free supply of different sprays, to help release dirt and improve the shine on a horse's coat.

A kit of her own would be a great birthday present addition, along with the riding lessons, she thought.

Eventually, Becky started to huff and puff.

"Can we go?" she said. "There's only so much pony stuff I can handle, you know. I'm ready to go now."

"Come on then," said Tilly. "I'm ready too."

But really she could have stayed in that shop for hours.

Eight

On Thursday, Tilly got a lift to Silver Shoe with Mia's mum. They met at the school gates at four o'clock as usual. In the car they all talked excitedly about Tilly's lesson while they got changed into their stable clothes. Tilly pulled on her pink polo shirt and a pair of cream jodhpurs that Cally had given her.

"I bet you're a natural!" said Cally.

"Definitely," said Mia. "You'll be riding with us in no time."

I hope so, thought Tilly.

When they got to the stables, Tilly went over to the sand school where Angela was waiting with Bunny, the dapple grey pony that Mia and Cally had been riding last week.

"Hi, Tilly. This is Bunny Hop. I think she'll be perfect for your first lesson. She's only 13hh and very experienced. Her owner, Zoe, is in America, so I'm sure Bunny will appreciate the attention. Come and say hello."

Tilly climbed over the fence of the sand school. Her feelings were a mixture of excitement and nerves. She'd never been on a horse before and didn't want to make any mistakes, but at the same time, she was

68

thrilled to be finally getting the chance.

Fortunately, Bunny looked reassuringly small and gentle. Angela checked Tilly's clothing and boots.

"You look great, so all you need is this," said Angela, handing Tilly a crash helmet with a black silk on it. "Try it on. If it doesn't fit I've got others."

Tilly fitted the hat to her head. It was just right. Angela adjusted the chin strap for her and tucked her plaits behind her shoulders.

"There. You look a proper young rider."

Tilly grinned from ear to ear. She wished her mum and dad could see her now.

"The first thing we need to do is learn how to mount. Once you're up and comfortable, we'll go for a little walk

69

around the school to give you a chance to get a feel for it. Does that sound okay?"

"Brilliant!" said Tilly.

Angela showed Tilly how to hold the reins and mane with one hand and the saddle with the other. Then she demonstrated how to place the ball of her foot into the stirrup and spring up and over with the other leg.

Angela made it look easy, but the first couple of times Tilly tried, she couldn't get enough lift. She stumbled back to the ground, frustrated with herself.

"Don't worry," said Angela. "That happens to everyone – you'll get used to it. Bunny won't mind how many times it takes. Try again. Really use your leg to lift yourself."

This time, following Angela's advice, Tilly managed to swing herself up and into the saddle in one smooth motion. It felt great. For a moment, she was so pleased with herself that she forgot to notice that for the first time ever, she, Tilly Redbrow, was actually sitting on a pony.

As Angela led Bunny around the school, Tilly concentrated on what her hands and feet and body were doing. She wanted to get everything right, but the effort was making her tense.

"Relax a bit," said Angela. "Get a feel for Bunny's movement beneath you. Good riding is all about balance and straightness. But if you try too hard you'll lose your natural sense of it. Bring your heels down in the stirrups and just think about sitting tall – as if a piece of string is attached to the top of your head, pulling you tall."

Tilly pushed her heels down and elongated her back. Immediately she felt more balanced and in control.

"That's it," encouraged Angela. "The majority of a horse's problems can usually be traced to a rider's poor position, so always focus on sitting straight and in balance. You'll get used to it with experience."

They walked several more circuits of
the sand school. Tilly had to keep
concentrating on the things that Angela had

taught her because they didn't come
automatically, but it felt good nonetheless.
They reached the fence and then Angela
unclipped the lead rope.

"I think you're ready to try a circuit by
yourself."

Tilly smiled and nodded, but inside
she was a little bit nervous.

"Just a nice gentle walk," reassured
Angela. "Try not to hold the reins
too tightly, but don't let them get
too long either – one of the
most common problems is
riders with too long a rein.
Try with your leg to nudge
her forward into a light
rein contact."

She showed Tilly how
to gather up a loop of rein close to
Bunny's mane, but Tilly found it
difficult to relax. Her forearms were
rigid.

"What if she runs away from me?"
she said anxiously.

73

"You'll be okay. Bunny knows what she's doing. She's very protective of her young riders. Think of your arm and the rein as a piece of elastic that runs straight through your hand to your elbow – your arm is like an extension of the rein. Bunny can feel the subtlest of movements along this piece of elastic, so the signals don't need to be over-exaggerated."

Tilly adjusted her grip and relaxed her arms. At the same time, she made an effort to sit up straight. It all seemed like a lot to remember, making her arms do one thing and her legs and back do another!

"Okay? Ready?"

Tilly nodded.

"Off you go."

Bunny walked on and Tilly could feel herself really riding. It wasn't anything like as fast and as graceful as she had imagined

74

in all those daydreams about galloping across the prairie on Magic Spirit. It wasn't easy, and it must have looked a bit clumsy, but it still felt amazing.

Nine

When the lesson was finished, Angela led them back to the stables where Duncan showed Tilly how to take off Bunny's tack.

"Every horse should have correctly fitting bridles and saddles," he explained. "So many people don't fit bridles properly. A horse's mouth is very sensitive and there's nothing worse than a bit that's hanging too low or too high. If the bit is the right size and in the right position, with the noseband sitting just below the cheekbone, then it

makes it much easier for the horse to take
an even contact from the rein."

He showed Tilly how to run up the
stirrups and then undo the girth. Before he
took the saddle off he showed her how to
fit it so that the pommel didn't sit too low
over the horse's wither.

"Good soft leather that. Let's take this
stuff back to the tack room, and I'll show
you how to clean and take care of
everything."

As they walked across the yard, Duncan
glanced sideways at Tilly.

"I saw you talking to Red Admiral by the way," he said quietly, as though it was a secret.

Tilly blushed.

"Whatever you said, or did, well, it seems to have helped. It's extraordinary how much better he seems – the heat and filling have totally disappeared from his leg. Jack Fisher thinks he'll make it to the Cosford race meeting. Doubts he'll win, but at least he'll get a run. So what's your secret, Tilly?"

Tilly shrugged, because truthfully she didn't know. She felt fabulous though. She'd had her first riding lesson and Red Admiral had made great progress. Could things get any better?

The tack room was warm and smelled of old leather. Tilly loved it. She stared in wonder at the rows of bridles and reins hung neatly

on the wooden-panelled walls in three rows,
and the different kinds of saddle racks on
another wall: eventing saddles, unusual
jumping saddles, dressage saddles. There
was a saddle horse in the centre of the room
and a hook where the bridles were cleaned
before being hung up in their correct places.
Duncan fetched a bucket of hot water and a
sponge, and then the pair of them were
ready to clean Bunny's tack.

"First of all, you need to remove any
grease and dirt with a hot damp cloth –
dirty tack can cause skin infections for the
horse. Careful cleaning gives you a good
chance to check the stitching and see that
nothing is damaged or worn out."

Tilly wiped the equipment with a cloth
and washed the bit and stirrup irons.

"Now use some saddle soap, which
keeps everything supple – here."

He passed Tilly a damp sponge, which
she rubbed across both sides of the saddle,
and then he showed her how to apply a
leather dressing on the underside.

"You only need to use leather dressing once a month. And obviously with synthetic tack, it isn't necessary at all."

"Do you think Magic Spirit will get his own tack?" she asked.

"Sure," said Duncan. "I'll have to start breaking him in soon. Although he's had some experience of being handled, he's got a long way to go before he's rideable. I think he'll be a tricky character to work with, but we'll see what we can do."

"Can I watch when you break him in?" asked Tilly eagerly.

"Watch? You'll be helping me, Tilly. Magic Spirit trusts you more than anyone. With your input I'm sure we'll eventually get a good response from him."

Suddenly the door of the tack room swung open. It was Cally and Mia returning from their ride, looking sweaty but pleased.

"Hey, Tilly! How was your lesson?"

"It was brilliant," said Tilly, buzzing.

"Bunny's a sweet little pony, isn't she?"

"She's lovely," Tilly replied, pleased

that she could talk from experience now.

"So when's your next lesson? You've got to hurry up and get good, so that you can come out with us!" said Mia.

"No one needs to hurry up anything," interrupted Duncan firmly. "Tilly will learn to ride in her own time. There's no need to rush."

"I know, I know," said Mia, playfully flicking his baseball cap. Cally kept quiet. She always did around Duncan. Tilly knew this was because she had a crush on him.

"But seriously, Tilly," added Mia. "When is your next lesson? We'll come and watch."

Tilly looked at the ceiling.

"Um, I don't know. It depends on whether my mum and dad agree to get me lessons for my birthday or not."

"Your birthday! You didn't tell us it was your birthday! When?"

"June the twenty-first."

"That's the day of the Cosford races," grinned Mia. "You'll have to join us – loads of people from Silver Shoe are going. We go every year – it's really fun and everyone gets dressed up. You're going to be racing, aren't you, Duncan?"

"That's right. You should definitely join us. I'm sure there'll be room in one of the cars for a little one," he said, smiling at Tilly.

Ten

When Tilly woke up on the twenty-first of June, she had a feeling that it would be a doubly good day. Not only because it was her birthday, but because she was going to the Cosford races to watch Red Admiral race.

Adam was the first to wish her a happy birthday, pouncing on her bed and singing:

"Happy birthday to you,
Squashed tomatoes and poo,
I saw a fat monkey,
And I thought it was you!"

At breakfast, Tilly opened her presents.
From Adam, she got the horseshoe earrings
she'd asked for. From her mum
and dad, she got a pair of
smart denim-look jodhpurs,
like the ones she'd seen in
the shop. She tried them on
and they fitted perfectly.

"Thanks, Mum. Thanks, Dad," she
said, kissing them both, and
admiring her reflection in the
mirror.

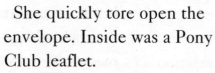

"There's one more
thing," said her dad, pulling
an envelope out of his pocket.

Tilly held her breath. Could this be the
riding lessons she'd been hoping for?

She quickly tore open the
envelope. Inside was a Pony
Club leaflet.

"We've bought you special
membership to the Cosford
branch," said her mum, smiling.
"Angela recommended it. She

said all the girls at Silver Shoe are members. They organise rallies and events, and during the school holidays they run special camps. You can borrow a pony from the stables. Won't that be fun?"

"That's ace. Thanks, Mum."

But although Tilly was thrilled with her Pony Club membership, she couldn't help worrying that the thing she wanted most of all had been forgotten about – riding lessons. She decided not to say anything, in case it made her mum and dad feel bad. They'd got her so many lovely things, it seemed greedy to ask for more. Instead, she studied the Pony Club leaflet and tried to put it out of her mind.

Tilly got a lift to the Cosford race course
with Mia's mum and dad, who were both
dressed glamorously and arguing about
which horses they were going to place bets
on. Tilly, Mia and Cally sat in the back
seat, discussing Duncan's tactics. He was
riding Red Admiral in the Cosford
Champion Hurdle.

When they arrived, the place was bustling with activity. Several huge marquees lined the track and there were hoards of smartly-dressed people chatting and laughing in groups and waving their race cards about.

Tilly and the girls made their way through the crowds and leaned up against the barrier so that they could get a good look at the race.

"It looks like a green velvet carpet!" gasped Cally. There wasn't a blade of grass out of place.

"Imagine flying those hurdles and galloping up to the finishing line – it would be like riding Pegasus!"

"Wow!" they all said together.

"Hello, girls," said a voice behind them. It was Angela. She was wearing a suit and had her hair pinned back with a flower clip. She looked very pretty.

"Hi, Angela."

"Where's Red Admiral?" said Cally excitedly. "Can we see him?"

"Not right now, I'm afraid. He's in the saddling enclosure. He'll be walked around the parade paddock in twenty minutes. They lead the horses around the paddock before a race so that everyone can view the runners and choose which ones they might place their money on."

"Is Duncan nervous?" asked Mia.

"No, well, at least, if he is, he doesn't show it."

"Do you think he and Red Admiral will win?" asked Tilly.

"Hmm, that's a tricky one. Red Admiral loves firm ground, so the dry weather will suit him. But he hasn't raced for a long time, so that will probably slow him down. We didn't think he'd make it for this race, but weirdly his leg has come right in the nick of time."

Tilly didn't say anything. She just twisted the horsehair bracelet she'd made from Red Admiral's tail and tried to send positive thoughts to him and Duncan.

"Come and join the Silver Shoe crowd

in the enclosure, girls. We've got a great view of the finish."

Tilly insisted she wanted to wish Red Admiral luck before the race, so she went to see him being led round the paddock by Jack. His coat was gleaming and he looked majestic. To top it all, he wore the number seven on his saddle cloth – Tilly's lucky number.

Suddenly a bell rang to signal to the jockeys that it was time to mount their horses. There were nerves all round. Jack hoped that Red was fit, plus this was the first race that Duncan was to ride for Silver Shoe Farm – something he had only ever dreamed about. The Brigdales, Red Admiral's owners, had kept their promise and allowed Red to stay at Silver Shoe Farm as a thank you for all the hard work that had gone into his rehabilitation.

The Brigdales were in the middle of the paddock with Duncan, who was wearing their familiar colours of green with a yellow cross and a white silk cap over his crash helmet. As the jockeys mounted Tilly could see the owners wishing them luck and the trainers giving them last words of advice.

Jack sensibly told Duncan to ride Red Admiral according to how he felt – not to push him hard, but if it felt good at the halfway point, to let him run. They circled the paddock one last time before going out onto the course.

Just as Tilly was regretting she hadn't wished Duncan or Red good luck, they stopped directly in front of her. Red affectionately nudged her arm and Tilly whispered to him, "Go like the wind, but above all, keep safe!" Then she looked up and wished Duncan luck.

By the time Tilly had caught up with everyone in the members' enclosure, the horses had cantered down to the start. There were lots of familiar faces from Silver Shoe Farm, all whispering and smiling and giving thumbs-up gestures. Jack Fisher was standing quietly at the side, his arms folded, a little apart from everyone else. Tilly tugged her bracelet and sent positive thoughts to him too.

The commentator announced that the horses were under starter's orders. A hush spread across the crowd and Tilly could feel the atmosphere bristle.

"Oh, crumbs!" whispered Mia. "It's *too* exciting."

She grabbed Tilly's hand and squeezed it. Cally, standing next to her, was jiggling up and down.

"Don't get your hopes up," said Mia's dad, who had stepped in behind them. "I've heard the Silver Shoe Farm horse is a non-starter."

"Shhh!" hissed Mia. "What do you

know about it anyway, Dad?"

"I know I've got thirty quid riding on it," he growled.

"Lucky Francis takes up the running!" said the commentator, as the horses approached the first flight of hurdles. They cleared it with ease and thundered onto the second flight. There were seventeen horses in the race and at this early stage Red Admiral lay mid-field travelling with ease.

Tilly couldn't believe how stylish Duncan looked, like a professional who had been racing for years. As the horses approached halfway, the crowd grew louder and louder, urging the horses they had bet on to run faster.

It upset Tilly to see a nasty fall at the sixth flight of hurdles, but thankfully both horse and rider were soon on their feet. She kept nervously twiddling her Red

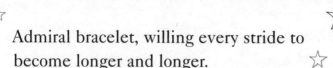

Admiral bracelet, willing every stride to become longer and longer.

With just two hurdles to go, she hoped he was in with a chance, but after hearing everyone's doubts, she knew it was unlikely they would win. She glanced over at Jack Fisher, who was chewing his nails, eyes glued to the course.

"Go on, Red Admiral! Go on, Duncan!" yelled Cally and Mia.

"Yes!" yelled Mia's dad, punching the air with his fist as Red Admiral started to come up through the field of runners.

It wasn't over yet. There was still one more flight of hurdles on the home straight. Red Admiral was neck and neck with a steely grey horse called Morning Frost. The commentator was shouting enthusiastically. The crowd was going wild as they cleared the last alongside each other.

He can't be beaten at this stage in the race, thought Tilly, closing her eyes.

"Come on, Red – faster, faster, you can

do it!" she bellowed at the top of her voice.

Instantly, as if Red had heard her, he surged forward lowering his head and neck. He galloped past Morning Frost and crossed the finishing line with a horse's length between them.

The sound of cheering followed and Tilly immediately opened her eyes. She could just about make out Duncan, smiling from ear to ear as he patted Red Admiral on the shoulder. It was good news!

The commentator announced the first three places. To hear the words: 'First: Red Admiral' was music to the ears of everyone at Silver Shoe Farm.

"Red Admiral is the winner of the seventeenth annual Cosford Champion Hurdle! What a horse!"

The Silver Shoe gang roared with delight. Mia's dad threw his programme into the air and started dancing around, singing

'Who wants to be a millionaire!' People everywhere were laughing and hugging each other.

In the corner, Tilly spotted Jack Fisher, standing alone and smiling to himself. She slipped through the happy crowd and approached him.

"Well done, Mr Fisher! You did it!" she said quietly.

"And well done to you, Tilly! You did it too!" he nodded, with a knowing glint in his eye.

Eleven

"I think this has been the best birthday ever," said Tilly, as they arrived back at Silver Shoe Farm, where she was expecting to be picked up by her mum and dad. She noticed their car was parked in the lane, but they were nowhere to be seen.

"It's not over yet," said Mia.

"What do you mean?" said Tilly.

"Um, do you think you could help us muck out Rosie's stall quickly? We didn't get a chance to do it this morning."

"Oh, er, yeah. I guess," said Tilly obligingly, although she wasn't exactly keen on the idea of shovelling manure after such a thrilling day.

"Thanks," said Cally and Mia together, eyes sparkling.

Tilly trudged over to the stables and picked up a fork and shovel. She was confused as to why Cally and Mia weren't coming to help her. And she couldn't help wondering where her mum and dad had disappeared to? Suddenly it seemed as though everyone was behaving oddly. Even Angela was rushing about and didn't stop to say hello.

She went into the tack room to fetch some water and a broom, and

104

when she came out the yard was empty.
She walked over to the stables, opened the
door and went inside.

"SURPRISE!" came a chorus of voices.

"Happy birthday, Tilly!"

The stable was lined with banners and
ribbons. Everyone, including Tilly's mum
and dad, and her best friend Becky,

were waving at her. They were wearing party hats, and some of the horses who didn't mind were wearing them too. Tilly laughed and put the fork down.

"Here, have some birthday cake," said Angela. "I made it myself – it was my mum's old recipe."

"We've even got a special cake for the horses," said Cally, pointing to an enormous slab of seeds and honey.

They all sat down on bales of hay and ate cake and drank homemade lemonade. The combination was delicious.

"So this is where you spend all your time," said Becky, smiling. "It's quite cool actually. Here, I got you this."

Becky handed Tilly a present. Tilly unwrapped it and inside was one of the grooming kits she'd admired in the riding shop.

"Thanks, Becky!"

"I thought you'd like it – after you drooled all over it in that shop!"

Tilly giggled.

Twenty minutes later, the sound of an engine purred in the yard.

"Hey! They're back!" said Mia.

Everyone got up and went outside, to where Duncan was leading Red Admiral out of the horse box. Angela rushed over and kissed Duncan on the cheek. Tilly, Mia and Cally nudged each other.

"I hear you were fantastic," said Mr Redbrow, smiling at Duncan as he patted Red Admiral on the shoulder.

"Oh, thanks, but it wasn't just down to me. I had a bit of help," he said, nodding at Tilly. "Happy birthday. Did you enjoy watching your first race?"

"It was brilliant!" said Tilly. "Here, I made you this."

She handed Duncan the horsehair bracelet she had made from Red Admiral's tail.

"Oh, thanks, Tilly. How thoughtful. So, what about you? Did you get those riding lessons you wanted?"

"Oh, um, not exactly," said Tilly,

awkwardly. "But that's okay," she shrugged, trying to hide her disappointment.

"Hang on a minute," said her dad suddenly. "I nearly forgot. Your other present, Tiger Lil'. . ."

"What other present?" asked Tilly.

"Ah ha," said Angela stepping forward. "Your parents and I have been doing some talking. We know how much you want riding lessons and, well, we've agreed that you can have as many as you need."

"But that will be so expensive for you," said Tilly, looking at her parents.

"It's okay," said her mum. "We'll pay for weekly lessons, and then Angela said she'd try to give you a bit of extra tuition for free. She thinks you've got such an extraordinary gift with the horses that it shouldn't be wasted."

"*Really?*" gasped Tilly.

"You'll have to work hard," said Angela cautiously. "But I know you won't mind that."

"Of course I won't," said Tilly, throwing

her arms around her mum and dad, and then Angela.

Mia and Cally clapped their hands together. They were almost as pleased as Tilly was.

"I was wrong when I said I think this has been the best birthday ever," said Tilly, stroking Red Admiral's nose.

"Actually, I know it's the best birthday ever!"

And with that, everyone cheered.

Pippa's Top Tips

Make sure the head collar is comfortable for your pony. When fitting it, always be careful to avoid their eyes, ears and nose, and don't make it too tight. Head collars are always fitted more loosely than bridles.

Horses can be unpredictable creatures, so you should always take care around them. For example, never loop the lead rope around your hand. If your pony pulls away suddenly, you risk injuring your hand.

Good riding is all about balance and straightness, and the majority of a horse's problems can usually be traced to a rider's poor position.

Always sit tall, as if a piece of string is attached to the top of your head, pulling you up.

Establish a light rein contact. Think of your arm and the rein as a piece of elastic that runs through your hand to your elbow. Your pony can feel the slightest of movements along the rein, so your signals don't need to be over-exaggerated.

A pony's mouth is very sensitive and there's nothing worse than an ill-fitting bit. The bit should be just the right size and position, with the noseband sitting just below the cheek bone.

Hosing your pony's leg can help reduce a swelling if he's taken a knock, but always get a vet to check out any injuries.

Dirty tack can cause skin infections for a horse, so always clean your tack after riding. First, remove any grease and dirt with a hot, damp cloth, then use some saddle soap to keep everything supple.

Careful cleaning also gives you a good chance to check the stitching and see that nothing is damaged or worn out. You should apply a leather dressing to the underside of the tack once a month – but, of course, this won't be necessary for synthetic tack.

Joining your local Pony Club is a great way to learn all the skills you need to care for your horse. They organise rallies and events, and some even run special camps during the school holidays.

For more about Tilly and Silver Shoe Farm –
including pony tips, quizzes and everything
you ever wanted to know about horses – visit
www.tillysponytails.co.uk

TILLY'S PONY TAILS

Magic Spirit
the
dream horse

TILLY'S PONY TAILS

Magic Spirit
the
dream horse

PIPPA FUNNELL

Illustrated by Jennifer Miles

Orion
Children's Books

First published in Great Britain in 2009
by Orion Children's Books
a division of the Orion Publishing Group Ltd
Orion House
5 Upper St Martin's Lane
London WC2H 9EA
An Hachette UK Company

5 7 9 8 6 4

ISBN 978 1 84255 709 9

Printed and bound in China

www.orionbooks.co.uk
www.tillysponytails.co.uk

For my dear father,
George Nolan

For more about Tilly and Silver Shoe Farm –
including pony tips, quizzes and everything
you ever wanted to know about horses –
visit www.tillysponytails.co.uk

One

"When I was a girl, about your age," said Tilly's mum, as she ran the brush through her daughter's long dark hair, "I was mad, absolutely mad, about ice skating."

Tilly turned her head, curious to know more.

"Ice skating?"

She tried to picture it: her mum at an ice rink, gliding gracefully on a pair of blades. Doing turns and jumps.

"Oh yes. I loved it," said Tilly's mum.
"Almost as much as you love horses, Tilly."

To say that Tilly Redbrow loved horses
was perhaps a bit of an understatement –
desperately, wildly, crazy about them more
like. You only had to take a peek in her
bedroom to see that she was horse and pony
mad. Every inch of wall space was covered
in posters of the best breeds from around
the world.

She spent as much
time as she could exploring
websites. Her favourites were
www.girlshorseclub.com and
www.ponybox.com. Here, she could read blogs
and manage her own online equestrian team,
losing herself in a world of horses
that was all hers.

Scattered over the floor of her room were copies of her favourite magazine, *Pony*, which her dad bought for her once a month, from the big newsagent in the next village.

Tilly liked to gaze at the photographs of other *Pony* readers. These were girls who really did have their own ponies: Helen Davis from Somerset and her dappled grey Connemara, Prince, jumping a water ditch; Lucy Nicholson from Oxford clearing a round on her 13hh pony, Featherboy. Tilly wished it could be her in the photos.

At night, when she lay in bed, just before falling asleep, she would imagine galloping across the open prairie, or through the countryside, being carried away by her favourite fantasy horse: a mysterious black stallion called Magic Spirit.

"Tilly! *Tilly*!" said her mum, bringing her back to reality. "Do you want bunches or plaits?"

"Plaits."

"Always plaits," said her mum, as she started weaving sections of Tilly's dark hair, which was too long for Tilly to do herself. She refused to get it cut. It had been long ever since she could remember. It reached all the way down her back, and it was a pain to wash and look after, but she liked it.

"So did you have your own ice-skates then?" Tilly asked, when her mum had finished.

"Goodness, no. Far too expensive. Nanny Gwen and Grandpa Pete couldn't afford luxuries like that, so I had to make do with watching it on the telly. All those lovely fluttering outfits and sequins . . . so pretty.

And I had lots of books and posters – just like you. I used to sit for hours looking at pictures of figure skaters and thinking to myself, why can't that be *me*? Oh well, too late now, I suppose. Silly ideas, eh?"

But in her heart, Tilly's mum knew they weren't just silly ideas.

She looked at Tilly's thoughtful reflection in the mirror, and knew how much her horse daydreams meant to her. She wondered how she could make these daydreams come true.

"How about some breakfast?" she said. "I've got some fresh bread from the bakers'. Maybe later we can make a cosy nest in the lounge, with blankets and cushions, and

watch *The Horse Whisperer* again?"

"Okay," said Tilly. "But I'd better take Scruff for a walk first."

Scruff was the Redbrow family's dog, a long-haired Jack Russell, and he was full of energy. The more exercise he got, the better. As soon as he heard the door opening he scampered towards Tilly, wagging his stubby tail.

Lower Norbury was a small place – a pub, a meeting hall and a post office, surrounded by a few stone cottages. Although it was much quieter than the nearby town of North Cosford, Tilly loved living there. She always enjoyed taking Scruff for walks down the main street on a sunny afternoon, smelling the flowers and listening to the birds.

Sometimes riders passed through, usually from Cavendish Hall, which was the exclusive boarding school and riding centre on the outskirts of North Cosford. Tilly had driven past it many times, stared up at its grand iron gates, longing to know what it was like inside. She'd heard that the pupils who went there were able to ride every day.

CAVENDISH
HALL
....
PRIVATE

No one from *her* school, Heathwell High
– where her dad taught – no one from there,
as far as Tilly knew, was remotely interested
in riding.

If only, she thought.

Suddenly three ponies emerged from the
lane: two chestnuts and a bay. Their riders

were all girls, about Tilly's age, dressed in neat jodhpurs and designer t-shirts, with sleek blonde ponytails flowing from under their riding hats. They were definitely Cavendish Hall girls.

Tilly and Scruff stopped to admire the ponies. The bay, in particular, moved gracefully and his silky coat glistened in the sunlight. What a beautiful, magnificent creature, she thought. As the pony passed by, he stopped and leaned his nose towards her, gently sniffing at the bracelet around her wrist. The rider immediately apologised:

"Sorry. Don't worry – he's usually very good-natured. He won't hurt you or anything."

"I know," said Tilly, smiling. She reached out to the pony and stroked the white star on his forehead. He moved towards her, and started nuzzling her hand, as though her touch was blissful and soothing.

"What's got into you, Blaze?" said the rider impatiently. "He doesn't normally fuss over strangers. I *am* sorry."

The other two ponies came up behind them, their riders whispering together.

"What's she doing?" whispered one of them, loud enough for Tilly to hear. "Come on. Let's go, or we'll be late for our dressage lesson."

With that, the group trotted on, leaving Tilly alone at the roadside. How lucky they are,

she thought, as she watched them disappear round the corner. And as she and Scruff ambled home, she kept asking herself, why can't that be me?

"So what's up, 'Tiger Lil'?" asked Mr Redbrow. He was the only person who called Tilly by her real name, Tiger Lily. He always knew when she was upset, because she would go very quiet and sit playing with her special bracelet.

"That old thing will break if you're not careful," he said, watching her twist it round and round her finger. It was strange looking, made from woven horsehairs – black, plaited like Tilly's hair, and linked with a small silver clasp. Tilly had worn the bracelet all her life. She'd had it since birth, but no one knew where it came from – and there was little chance of finding out, because when she was very young, Tilly had been adopted.

For as long as Tilly could remember, she'd been a Redbrow, and was happy to be so; but that didn't stop her from sometimes wondering who her mother and father were. And who *she* really was. The horsehair bracelet was her only link to the past, but it couldn't tell her anything.

Despite being happy with the Redbrow family, Tilly knew she was different. For a start, her thick, dark hair and olive skin made her stand out. Everyone in her adoptive family was fair and freckly, with tall, solid figures. Tilly was small and delicate. Her brother, Adam, who was born three years

after the Redbrows had adopted Tilly, was
taller than her already.

Tilly loved Adam, but he got on her
nerves too. He was noisy and messy, and
always hogged the computer. He would
spend hours playing *Dungeons and Dragons*
when Tilly wanted to chat online, or look up
new pony websites. And he had an annoying
habit of rushing to the computer table, just
when he thought Tilly might do the same.

Tilly's dad sat down on the step and began
tickling Scruff's ears.

"Did you see those three lovely ponies go
through the village today?" he asked, hoping
this would cheer her up.

Tilly just stared at her trainers and nodded.

"I was talking to Tom Cracknell from the
post office earlier. He said that the girls who
ride them are three of the best junior show
jumpers in the county. They go to Cavendish

Hall and practise every day after school. There's been quite a lot of chatter about them in the local paper. Perhaps we should go along one day and watch them practise?"

"Everyone always goes on about the Cavendish Hall girls," said Tilly sulkily. "They're probably not *that* good."

"Oh, come on, Tiger Lil', don't be like that – what have they got that you haven't, eh?"

Their own ponies, for a start, thought Tilly.

Two

The following day, Tilly and her mum were driving through the winding lane towards North Cosford. They were in a hurry to get to the supermarket on the edge of town, and then back in time to get dinner ready. But as soon as they turned onto the high street, their journey came to a halt. A line of cars was blocking the way.

"What is it?" complained Mrs Redbrow. "There's never usually traffic at this hour. Goodness, it's getting late."

They sat for a while and Tilly stared out of the window, imagining how it would feel to escape from this standstill, to gallop away on Magic Spirit – no saddle, the wind all about her, completely free. She sighed to herself.

Suddenly they heard shouts from down the street. There was a lot of commotion, and people calling to each other.

"Perhaps we should turn back and go the long way round?"

"No wait. Something's happening," said Tilly. She leaned out of the window.

Ahead of them, a familiar shape was moving to and fro.

"What is it?" said her mum.

"It looks like a horse. It's trapped in the road, and everyone's crowding round and bothering it," said Tilly, concerned.

There were more shouts, and a mother and two children came running along the pavement. The horse started to rear and whinny, terrified, its eyes rolling alarmingly.

"I've got to help," cried Tilly, leaping out of the car.

"Tilly! Come back!" shouted Mrs Redbrow. "Get back here! Don't be silly – it could be dangerous!"

But it was too late. Her daughter was already halfway down the street, running in the opposite direction to everyone else.

The horse was thin. His mane was matted and his grey coat was covered in scratches and sores. He was clearly very distressed, dripping with sweat and shaking like a jelly. As soon as anyone tried to approach him, he would rear up on his hind legs with his ears flat back. But Tilly knew that he was acting out of fear rather than anger. He wasn't trying to hurt anyone. He was frightened.

A bald man in a blue suit tried to pull her away. He was shouting, telling everyone to get back – but Tilly understood that the shouting was only making the distraught horse more upset.

"Someone call the police," the man yelled. "This crazy horse is going to kill someone if we don't get it under control!"

Tilly realised what she had to do. Suddenly everything around her seemed to fade and go quiet, as if the rest of the world had disappeared. All that remained was her and the horse.

She stepped quietly beside him, careful not to look directly into his eyes. And then she stood calmly, until he became aware of her. Somehow, her presence made him still.

He stopped snorting, stopped swishing his tail and moved towards her.

"That's it, good boy," she said softly, as he lowered his head. "That's it, Magic Spirit. Don't worry. I'm Tilly. I'll help you. There boy, good boy."

With his head lowered, he allowed her to rub his nose. She felt his hot breath on her hands and saw the sadness in his eyes. He nibbled her sleeve and sniffed around her special bracelet, until slowly she was able to reach her hand up and take hold of his tatty

rope halter. Then, gently, she led him away, off the roadside and into the shelter of a nearby empty car park.

Twenty minutes later, after the crowds and traffic had cleared, a young woman arrived in a four-wheel drive towing a trailer. She got out, and after checking the horse for injuries, came straight over to Tilly.

"You must be the girl who saved the day. I've heard what an amazing job you did."

"Are you from Cavendish Hall?" asked Tilly excitedly.

"Oh no. My father and I own a yard a few miles from here called Silver Shoe Farm. We're a busy livery yard with all sorts of horses, from ponies to competition horses. We have young ones, and even the odd rehab racehorse. You know, racehorses who need time and care to recover from their injuries."

The woman smiled. "I'm Angela, by the way."

I'm Tilly . . . short for Tiger Lily," said Tilly, knowing instantly that they were going to get on well.

"What will happen to the horse?" she asked. "His name's Magic Spirit . . . I think."

"Hmm, that's a good name. That's what we'll call him then. Well, no one seems to know where he came from. I assume someone must have abandoned him in one of the fields, and judging by his condition, I'm afraid it looks like he's had a pretty horrible

30

time. I'll take him back to Silver Shoe Farm
and see what we can do. Part of what we do
is help World Horse Welfare, who look
after unwanted or cruelly treated horses.
That's why I'm here to collect this poor boy.
Thanks for your help, Tilly. It's quite
incredible what you did, you know. Do you
spend a lot of time with horses?"

Tilly looked at the ground. "Sort of," she
muttered.

Angela looked surprised. "Well, you've
obviously got a natural way with them."

"Tilly's pony mad,"
said her mum, coming
to join them and
standing proudly beside
her. "She's got a room
full of books and
magazines."

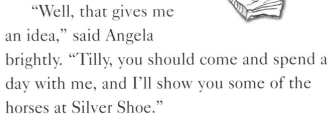

"Well, that gives me
an idea," said Angela
brightly. "Tilly, you should come and spend a
day with me, and I'll show you some of the
horses at Silver Shoe."

"*Really?*" gasped Tilly. "Can I?"

"Absolutely."

"And will I be able to help?"

"Of course," said Angela. "A special talent like yours shouldn't be wasted on books and magazines."

Three

All Tilly thought about for the rest for the week was her day at Silver Shoe Farm, which was arranged for Saturday. The time in between couldn't go fast enough. She sat through school, daydreaming about Magic Spirit and wondering if he was okay. Her Geography teacher had to repeat her name four times before he could get her attention.

And her best friend, Becky, said it was as if
she was on another planet: Planet
Pony.

When Saturday finally came,
Tilly was awake at six in the
morning. She lay in bed and
checked through her latest copy of
Pony, looking for ideas about grooming
and handling – making sure a horse is tied

before grooming
it; caring for
its hooves.
She wanted to
impress Angela
with her
knowledge.

After a bowl of
muesli and banana,
Tilly's favourite
breakfast, her dad
drove her to the
farm. At first they
missed the turning,
because the lane was
half hidden by leafy, overhanging tree
branches. It was like a secret hide-away.

When they finally found it, and saw the
sign for Silver Shoe Farm, Tilly could feel
butterflies in her stomach. They drove up an
avenue of silver birches until they reached
open fields for as far as the eye could see.
In the middle of these fields was a group of
cream buildings with reddish slate roofs, and

a couple of newly-creosoted black wooden barns.

"This must be it," said Mr Redbrow.

"It's perfect," whispered Tilly.

Angela met them in the yard, which was bustling with activity. There were three long stable blocks organised around a square patch of grass. Some of the horses were leaning their heads out, waiting for someone to give them some attention or, if they were lucky, the odd titbit. Others were being tacked up, or led through the yard, keen on the idea of having a few hours out in the paddocks.

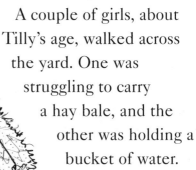

A couple of girls, about Tilly's age, walked across the yard. One was struggling to carry a hay bale, and the other was holding a bucket of water.

They looked at her
and smiled.

"That's Cally
and Mia," said
Angela. "They're here
every weekend. We're
a friendly bunch. You'll
definitely be made to feel
welcome at Silver Shoe. I've told everyone
about you. Let me show you around, and
then I'll introduce you to some of our horses
and people."

Tilly said goodbye to her dad, and didn't
feel at all nervous about being left without
him. She and Angela walked the length of
the yard, and Angela explained that they had
twenty stables and thirty acres for grazing.

"We've also got lots of woodland nearby,
which is great for hacking. Behind us is the
tack room, and that little building next to it
is the club room – where the gang like to
chill out at the end of the day. And over
there," she said, pointing to a large building
beyond the stables, "we have an indoor

menage for the winter months, and a big outdoor training area, with a gallop for the racehorses and eventers – that's where all the best stuff happens."

"Like what?" asked Tilly.

"Why don't you come and see for yourself?"

The outdoor arena was a huge grass area, lined with trees, with a sand school and a smaller pen for lunging, surrounded by wooden fencing.

"There's Red Admiral," said Angela. "He's a young thoroughbred. He's been injured recently; it's going to be a long time before he sees a racecourse."

They stopped at the fence and watched the proud chestnut-red horse being led round the pen. Eventually his handler, an old man in a checked shirt, brought him over to say hello.

"So, you must be Tilly," he said. "Very pleased to meet you. I'm Jack Fisher, Angela's father. I'm the owner of Silver Shoe – if you need anything, just come and ask. Angela's told me all about your efforts with that rescue horse the other day. Quite impressive."

"You mean Magic Spirit?" said Tilly, glancing between him and Angela. "Where is he? Can I see him? Is he doing okay?"

"He's . . . um . . . he's having a bit of a hard time, Tilly," said Angela slowly. The tone of her voice was worrying.

"He's a tricky character all right," added Jack Fisher. "But it's not unusual for rescue horses to be difficult, especially if they've been treated badly. We've had to keep him in a separate barn – he's kicked all the walls and chewed the wood. He hates the other horses and he won't take human contact.

40

Every time someone has tried to get near, he's reared. It's been almost a week and I desperately want to get him wormed and vaccinated, but at the moment he's too dangerous."

"I could help," said Tilly. "I think he trusts me – I could reassure him."

"Oh, I don't know about that," said Jack, swatting a fly away. "We promised your dad we'd look after you – we can't just send you into a barn with a traumatised animal. That's a crazy idea."

Tilly was frustrated.

"There's something about this girl though, Dad," Angela urged quietly. "Honestly, she's got a special way from what I've heard. I reckon we should at least try – for Magic Spirit's sake. Don't worry, I'll make sure she's safe and we won't take any chances."

"You'll drive me to an early grave one of these days," muttered Jack, rubbing his head. Red Admiral started to snort impatiently. "Look, I've got to get back to work with him. You girls go over to the barn

and do what you can for Magic Spirit, but any sign of trouble and you're straight out of there, right?"

"Right," they both said together, smiling.

Four

Magic Spirit was in a small black wooden barn at the end of the yard.

"Well, he's quiet at least," said Angela. "In the night he was whinnying and banging constantly. We could hear him from the house."

She and Tilly peered inside. The stall was dark, and at first Tilly couldn't see anything, then she saw the flash of his eyes. He was looking at her from the shadowy corner.

"Hello, Magic," she murmured. "It's me

again. It's Tilly.
Don't be
frightened."

Magic snorted
and shuffled through
the wood-chip bed
that had been laid
down for him, then he
stepped forward inquisitively.

"Can I go in?" asked Tilly, looking at
Angela.

"In a minute. See how he is first.
Remember what my dad said – no one's been
able to get near him yet, so we mustn't take
any risks. It looks like he's eaten some of his
hay at least."

Tilly leaned over the door of the barn and
reached out her hand, so that Magic, when he
was ready, could come and greet her. A minute
passed, and then slowly he came closer.

"Hello there," said Tilly in a soft voice,
as she stroked his nose. Magic started
sniffing at her bracelet, as he'd done the first
time they'd met each other.

44

"That's amazing," whispered Angela, watching from behind. "Amazing."

After a while, Tilly unbolted the bottom half of the stable door.

"I don't think you should do that," cautioned Angela. But in her typical determined way, Tilly had already made up her mind. She pulled the wooden door just wide enough for her to slip inside. Then she waited. She didn't go in immediately, because she knew that Magic would let her know exactly when he was ready for her to enter his space. He stepped backwards and rubbed his head against the stable wall. Tilly could see the splinters in the wood panels where he'd tried to kick through.

Eventually, she crept into the entrance and stood beside him. He allowed her to stroke his neck and shoulder. She was careful not to touch any sore patches, or make any sudden movements that would frighten him. This was something she knew about from reading lots of pony care books, but she had a different kind of knowledge as well. There was a special connection between them – something that

couldn't be learned from any book.

Outside, by the door, Angela was watching, her mouth open.

"Maybe I should call the vet right away," she said to herself. "Maybe Tilly can keep him calm while he gets checked over."

She reached into her pocket for her mobile phone.

Moments later, Jack Fisher entered the yard, leading Red Admiral, the haughty young thoroughbred. They had finished their training for the morning.

"Quick," Angela called over to Jack, in a loud whisper. "Come and look at this."

Jack crossed the yard, with Red at his side. They stopped a few feet from the stable and glanced in.

"Well I'll be blown," said Jack. "In all my
years of . . . I don't quite believe it . . . you
said the girl had a special knack but *this* is
extraordinary!"

Unaware of their audience, Tilly and
Magic carried on getting to know one
another. Tilly could see that despite his
scruffy appearance and bony body, Magic was
a tall, athletic-looking horse. In an instant,
she imagined that he'd make a great show
jumper; she saw herself riding him at
Olympia, skilfully clearing the biggest
fences. Magic Spirit nodded, as if he was
reading her thoughts and agreeing.

Suddenly, a gust of wind blew an empty
shavings bag across the yard, startling Red.
He spooked and shot
forward, snorting.
Magic instantly
leaped towards the
door, his ears
flat back,
baring his
teeth.

Shocked, Tilly stumbled away from him, nearly falling flat on her back. She picked herself up and got out of the way as quickly as she could. Her heart was beating faster than ever. Angela took hold of her arm and pulled her to safety, then shut the barn door.

Meanwhile, Jack was busy trying to settle Red Admiral.

"Goodness me," said Angela, brushing straw from Tilly's jacket. "Are you okay? You're not hurt are you? I'm so sorry . . . we should never have let you—"

Tilly took a deep breath.

"I'm all right. Honestly. It wasn't his fault. He was frightened."

But Tilly was shaking all over. Her hands were trembling, and no matter how much she tried to relax, she couldn't stop them.

"Oh dear," said Angela, frowning. "Let's go and have a nice hot drink. I think we need one."

Five

The clubroom was warm and cosy
with scruffy, comfy sofas and a
little kitchen area. Across the
walls were photos of riders and
their horses, either jumping,
racing or holding trophies.
Tilly noticed one of Angela,
standing proudly beside a
winning horse. On the far
side of the room, there was a notice-
board, which had rosettes pinned to it and

several notes advertising second-hand riding gear, hay for sale, and paddocks to let.

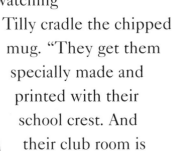

Tilly looked around while Angela made them hot chocolate. She added marshmallows and carried them over to the sofa.

"There you go," she said, passing Tilly a mug. It was chipped, but Tilly didn't mind.

"At Cavendish Hall they have designer mugs, you know," said Angela, watching Tilly cradle the chipped mug. "They get them specially made and printed with their school crest. And their club room is

52

really smart – it's got a surround sound TV and a DVD player and power showers."

"I like it here," said Tilly.

"Good," said Angela, relieved. "I'm glad – and I'm also glad," she added, raising her eyebrows and scraping back her long, red hair, "that you weren't hurt by Magic Spirit. No matter how well you get on with the ponies here, Tilly, you've got to remember that they can be unpredictable sometimes. I'll get the girls to go through the rules of safe handling with you, and then maybe you can help with some of the grooming and mucking out. How would that be?"

"Great!"

Just then, the two girls Tilly had seen in the yard earlier walked in. Both of them were busy texting on their mobiles, then they went straight to the kitchen to make themselves a drink.

"Cally. Mia. Come over and meet Tilly. She's visiting for the day."

They both turned and smiled.

"Hiya," they said together.

"Hi," said Tilly shyly.

"Hey, I recognise you," said Cally. "You go to Heathwell High, don't you? We're in the year above you – Miss Bright's form. Do you want a biscuit?"

She offered Tilly a packet of biscuits.

"Thanks," said Tilly.

"So have you got a pony, then?" asked Mia, sitting down beside them. She was small, with pale skin and short blonde hair. Cally was taller, and had lots of black curls and train-track braces on her teeth.

"No," said Tilly. "Have you?"

"Well, sort of. Me and Cally share one – we've been best friends for ever, and our mums decided it would be more affordable that way. We share all the expenses—"

"And all the work," added Cally.

"And then we both get to ride her – not at the same time of course!"

"You're so lucky," said Tilly.

"You'll have to come and meet her. She's lovely – her name's Rosie. Would that be okay, Angela? Can we take Tilly to see Rosie? We're about to groom her."

"Why not?" said Angela. "Don't forget the safety rules though, girls."

Tilly finished her hot chocolate and followed the girls back to the yard.

"First things first," said Mia sensibly, leading Tilly to the tack room. "If you're working close to a horse or pony, always wear sturdy boots.

Your trainers won't give you any protection if they tread on your feet!"

Tilly looked at her trainers.

"I've only got these," she said.

"Don't worry. I've got a spare pair you can borrow."

She handed Tilly a pair of brown jodhpur boots. Tilly pulled them on. They were the right size.

"Have them if you like," shrugged Mia. "They don't fit me anymore."

"Wow! Thanks."

They walked over to Rosie's stall, and Tilly loved the feeling of wearing the boots – they made her feel like a proper horsewoman. Cally opened the stable door and started making clucking noises. Rosie leaned her head out and began to nuzzle Cally's neck. She looked very friendly – a strawberry roan – but Tilly couldn't help feeling a little bit anxious after what had happened with Magic Spirit.

Mia carried a grooming kit over.

"She loves being groomed," she said. "We do it as often as we can because it keeps her coat nice and healthy – and it makes her look beautiful. But most of all, she likes the attention! She's such a princess!"

Rosie lowered her head.

Cally checked the headcollar.

"Is she safely tied?" asked Tilly, remembering what she'd read about in *Pony* magazine that morning.

"Yep. Safe and sound," replied Cally.

"But we always use a quick-release knot," added Mia. "So that she can pull free if she gets scared. Some horses don't like the feeling of being constrained and it makes them panic."

She reached into the grooming kit box and pulled out a brush. Tilly recognised it as a Dandy brush: a stiff-bristled brush used to loosen dirt. Mia started rubbing the Dandy in circular motions across Rosie's body, being very gentle around her thinner-skinned and bony areas. She talked to Rosie the whole time, whispering nice things and telling her how beautiful she was.

"We start at the top of the neck and then work our way down to her rear, and then switch sides – if she was covered in thick mud we'd use a plastic curry comb," explained Cally.

"Once all the dirt is loose, we comb her mane and tail, and then we use the softer bristled brush to get rid of the dirt. We scrape that brush with a metal curry comb to get the grease and dust out."

Once Cally had done all of this, she picked up an old tea towel.

"This is a stable rubber – it removes any remaining scurf and smoothes her coat. It makes her coat look super shiny. Then we'll use a comb for her mane and tail, and conditioning spray, which makes the comb glide through her tail. Do you want a go?"

Tilly took the brush in her hand and allowed it to glide across Rosie's body. As she did this, a beautiful sheen appeared on the pony's coat. Then Cally took the body brush and showed Tilly how to groom Rosie's face, making sure not to bother her eyes or the sensitive

bits around her nose and ears.

"And finally," said Mia. "We check her legs and clean her hooves."

Carefully, she ran her hands down Rosie's legs, feeling for any cuts or swellings. "It's important because if you get straight on and ride without checking, you could cause more damage, or even lameness.

"One of Angela's rules is that we always pick the horses' feet out with a hoof pick before coming out of the stable

– it keeps the yard tidier and Angela likes that. If the horses are turned out it's the first thing we do when we bring them in."

Just then Angela popped her head over the stable door. "How are you getting on?" she asked. "Have you remembered to paint her hooves with the special hoof oil? Tilly, did the girls tell you we keep a notebook in the tackroom listing all the dates of when our horses were last shod – normally a set of shoes lasts for five to six weeks."

Tilly watched, trying to take in all this new information and eager to have a go herself. One day Magic Spirit might let me groom *him*, she thought.

Before Tilly left Silver Shoe Farm that day, she made sure she paid one last visit to Magic Spirit. At first she was nervous, because of what had happened earlier, but she knew that if she let her worry get the better of her, it would make Magic Spirit nervous too. She leaned over the bottom half of the stable door and reached her hand in. To her relief, he was calm and gentle with her. He came over and let her stroke his neck, and gradually she started to scratch harder. He nuzzled the back of her neck.

"You scratch my back and I'll scratch yours," Tilly giggled, as Magic tickled her, sending goosebumps down her spine.

"Good boy," she said quietly. "Don't worry, I'll be back soon – I hope."

Then her mobile buzzed. It was her dad, texting to let her know that he was waiting in the lane for her. Time to go home.

Angela was in the yard, helping Cally and Mia to saddle up Rosie.

"Well, I hope you enjoyed yourself, Tilly," she said.

Tilly had had a great time, but when she looked at Rosie she also wished she'd had a chance to do some actual riding. Sensing this, Angela smiled.

"You'll have to come back soon, and maybe we'll get you up on one of the ponies . . ."

Tilly grinned.

"And you're welcome to help us groom Rosie again," said Cally.

Rosie fluttered her eyelashes.

"Cool."

"We'll see you on Monday," said Mia.

For a moment Tilly was puzzled, then she remembered that they went to the same school.

"Yes. See you then," said Tilly, as she opened the five-bar wooden gate, and climbed into the passenger seat of Mr Redbrow's car. He'd been sitting doing the crossword while he waited for her to say her goodbyes. Adam was in the back, eyes fixed on his Gameboy.

"Well?" said Mr Redbrow. "How was it then?"

"Aaah!" sighed Tilly, sinking into her seat and smiling. "Where do I start?"

Six

Tilly talked and thought about nothing but Silver Shoe Farm for the next few days. At supper on Saturday, it was the latest colours for jodhpurs. At breakfast on Sunday, it was hoof picks and body brushes. At lunchtime, it was how to catch a difficult horse. And in the evening, it was back to jodhpurs. Tilly was in her element. Her mum and dad were pleased, but by the fourth time they'd heard her detailed descriptions of Magic Spirit, Red Admiral and Rosie, they were somewhat worn out.

"You know," said Mrs Redbrow, when
Tilly had gone to bed. "She's so crazy about
ponies – it would be great if we could organise
some riding lessons for her. She'd be thrilled."

"I'd better go for that promotion then,"
said Tilly's dad, smiling.

On Monday morning, Tilly's best friend,
Becky, called for her. They walked to the bus
stop, to catch the 275 to school. On the
journey, as usual, they listened to music on
Becky's iPod, sharing the headphones as they
sang along.

"Did you watch *The X Factor* on
Saturday? Who did you think was best?"
asked Becky.

"I didn't watch any television this
weekend. I was busy. I was at Silver Shoe
Farm – *all* day," said Tilly.

"Ooh. Big deal," said Becky, pulling a
face and adjusting her headphone.

Becky had been Tilly's best friend ever since primary school. She didn't share Tilly's mad passion for ponies – she thought it was crazy, and liked to wind Tilly up. Tilly, in turn, liked to wind Becky up about her obsession with winning *The X Factor* and joining a girl band. But even though the girls had different interests they always had fun together and that's what mattered most of all.

The last lesson of the day was History. Tilly stared out of the window and wondered how she could help Angela and Magic Spirit. She remembered that she had the latest copy of *Pony* in her bag. When no one was looking, she pulled it out and slipped it in front of her textbook, so that she could read it while pretending to do her work.

She turned straight to the problem page, where readers had written in asking for advice, and soon she was lost in ideas about saddlery and training tips. She studied a letter from a girl who kept falling off her pony whenever he bucked. She wanted to know how to stay on. Tilly tried to imagine what she would do in that situation – get my legs forward, sit back, and stick like glue, she thought, just like cowboys at Rodeos. And to her surprise and pleasure, that's what the reply to the letter suggested too!

Moments later, Tilly felt a sharp jab in her ribs. It was Becky, warning her that Mr Baxter, the History teacher, was coming over.

He wasn't impressed.

"Tilly Redbrow! That doesn't look like
the Norman Conquest to me! Hand it over,
please!"

Tilly gave her teacher the magazine. She
could feel everyone in the class looking at
her. Mr Baxter leafed through it, turned his
nose up, and then marched over to his desk
and placed it in one of the drawers. Two boys
in the back row started whispering Tilly's
name and making stupid neighing noises.

"Ignore them," whispered Becky.

After the bell, Tilly waited at Mr Baxter's desk and asked for her magazine.

"I'll give it back to you, Tilly, but I'm not best pleased. How will you pass your exams if you don't pay attention in class? As a punishment, I want you to write five hundred words on the history of equestrianism. Got that? Five hundred words. Equestrianism. On my desk by tomorrow morning."

"Absolutely!" said Tilly, smiling. That's not a punishment, she thought.

Tilly and Becky caught the bus home. Sometimes they got a lift with Tilly's dad, but he often had to stay late for meetings. The girls walked through the village, picking leaves from the trees as they went and talking about Mr Baxter's funny hair. Becky was convinced he wore a wig. Tilly thought it was a hair transplant.

"Do you want to come round to mine?" asked Becky. "We could do our homework together, then go on the Nintendo DS. My brother's got a new game. He'll let us borrow it if he's in a good mood."

"I can't tonight," said Tilly. "I promised Baxter I'd write that horse essay."

"You're not *really* going to do that are you? He won't remember by the morning!"

"But I want to," said Tilly.

"Suit yourself."

They said goodbye and went their separate ways.

When Tilly got home, she made herself a hot chocolate and went straight to the computer. She printed some information from a website called www.horsesmart.co.uk, and then sat at the kitchen table and worked on her essay until it was dark, using her best handwriting and decorating the margins with drawings of ponies.

The horse research took up so much space that Mr Redbrow had to take his marking into the living room when he got home, and Mrs Redbrow was forced to prepare the supper on the tiniest square of tabletop. She kept smiling to herself though, because she'd never seen Tilly take so much care over homework before.

The following morning, Tilly took her essay straight to Mr Baxter. As Becky had predicted, he seemed confused when she handed it to him.

"Five hundred words on the history of equestrianism," said Tilly, out of breath because she'd run all the way to his classroom. "Except – I hope you don't mind – but it's not five hundred words, it's more like a thousand."

Mr Baxter just scratched his head and nodded.

Seven

Next day at school, Tilly went to find Becky in the lunch queue, so they could sit together as always. As she made her way between the canteen tables, she heard her name being called. The voice was familiar. She turned and looked.

"Tilly! Tilly! Over here!"

It was Cally. Mia was with her. They were both sitting at the long table, eating jacket potatoes. Tilly walked over.

"Come and sit with us," they said, smiling.

"Oh . . . I don't know if I can," said Tilly
anxiously, looking back at the queue where
Becky was waiting for her. She really wanted
to sit with Cally and Mia, but she didn't want
Becky to feel left out. In the end she
hovered at the end of the table, twiddling
one of her plaits.

"Guess what?" said Mia excitedly.

"Thanks to you, Angela was able to get the vet to look at that new rescue horse."

"You mean Magic Spirit?" said Tilly, wide-eyed.

"Yeah, after you visited him on Saturday, he was really calm – the calmest he's been since he arrived at the stables. He obviously trusts you. The vet checked him over and says he'll be okay."

"He's been vaccinated and wormed, and treated for his sores, and now he needs lots of feeding up," added Cally. "But with a bit of love and care we'll get him right. Angela never turns a horse away. Even though she loves training thoroughbreds, she'll help any animal. Hey, when are you coming to the farm again? Don't you miss Magic Spirit?"

"Come with us after school," said Mia. "My mum picks us up and drops us off at the stables every evening. She won't mind giving you a lift too."

Tilly felt overwhelmed. She couldn't stop smiling.

"If that's okay . . . that would be great, thanks."

"Cool. We'll meet you at the front gates, four o'clock. See you then."

Tilly walked away and went to find Becky, who had already got her lunch and was sitting at their favourite table, beneath the big window. She was prodding a lump of green jelly with the end of her spoon, and staring into space.

"There you are," she said, as Tilly joined her. "I thought you'd abandoned me."

And although Becky said it jokingly, there was something in the way she said it that made Tilly feel guilty.

At five to four, Tilly met her dad as he was walking from the Maths block.

"Can I go to Silver Shoe with Cally and

Mia?" she said breathlessly. "Mia's mum can give me a lift—"

"I suppose so," said her dad, almost dropping a pile of textbooks. "Make sure you're back in time for tea."

Tilly ran all the way to the front entrance. She felt relieved that Becky had already disappeared to the music department for her weekly singing lesson.

Cally and Mia were standing at the gates, busily texting on their mobiles, as usual. They greeted Tilly and then the three of them climbed into a huge midnight blue four-wheel drive.

Mia's mum was driving. She was young looking and very glamorous, with a stylish bob and long fingernails. Not like a mum at all, thought Tilly – more like a big sister.

"How was work?" said Mia, then she looked at Tilly and explained. "My mum owns a hair salon in North Cosford. It's called Dream Cuts. Do you know it?"

"No. My mum cuts my hair," said Tilly, embarrassed.

"Well, you've got lovely hair," said Mia's mum. "I can tell it's really thick and healthy. I reckon it would look nice with some layers – make you look a bit older."

Tilly blushed. Meanwhile, Cally and Mia started rummaging through a sports bag, pulling out jeans and t-shirts and changing into them.

"We're not allowed to go to the stables in our uniform," moaned Cally. "In case we get mucky. Here, you can borrow this," she said, handing Tilly a pale pink polo shirt.

They arrived at Silver Shoe Farm and Tilly felt the same rush of excitement she'd had the first time she saw it, appearing out of the fields, through the tunnel of trees. It was

a lovely evening – late April, and the trees were fresh with blossom and leaves.

The stable yard was busy. Two small ponies were having their manes pulled. And on the other side of the yard, there were some bigger horses being tacked up. The horses seemed to like each other's company and the atmosphere was very friendly. Tilly spotted Angela straightaway. Her wild red hair made her stand out. As soon as she noticed the three girls she came over.

"Hello, you lot. How nice to see you again, Tilly. Magic Spirit will be pleased. I suppose the girls have told you the good news about the vet. We're delighted with the progress Magic's making. He's definitely eating well. Doesn't seem to want to come out of his barn though. Oh well, we'll give it time."

She looked at Mia and Cally.

"Rosie's in the paddock. She was turned out after you groomed her this morning. She's had a nice day grazing with some of the other ponies. If you go and find Duncan, he'll help you catch her. Which of you is riding today?"

"*Me!*" they both said together,
exchanging looks.

"Oh, okay then.
I suppose it's Cally's
turn," said Mia
reluctantly.

"I went out yesterday.
Come on, Tilly, let's go
and see Magic Spirit."
She linked her arm through
Tilly's and swept her across the
yard, towards the small barn, while Cally
went to the tack room to get ready for her
ride.

"Who's Duncan?" asked Tilly.

"He's Angela's head
boy. He helps her run the
stables. He's a great jockey
– Angela says he's got real
stickability. He helps her

with all the young
horses. Cally really
fancies him, although
she'll tell you that she
doesn't!"

Tilly peered inside
the barn. Mia stayed
back.

Magic Spirit was in
the shadows, munching
hay. It was good to see
he had an appetite back.
He saw Tilly and
stepped forward.
Cautiously, he dipped
the tip of his nose
outside, as though he
was testing the air. Tilly
reached up her hand
and let him sniff it. She
gently told him she was
pleased to see him.

"You're so brave,"
said Mia admiringly.

"When I know a horse is likely to get freaked out, it makes me nervous."

"That's the thing," said Tilly, scratching Magic Spirit's neck. "I think he can sense our feelings – if we feel confident around him, he'll feel confident around us."

Eight

Over the next few days, Tilly couldn't wait to visit Silver Shoe Farm again. She swapped phone numbers with Cally and Mia, and on Thursday evening she got a text saying:

ME AND CAL GOING 2 STABLES TOMOZ B4 SCHOOL.
WANNA COME? PICK U UP AT 7. MIA. X

Tilly was too excited to worry about getting up early. She was out of bed before her alarm went off.

Mia's mum picked her up and drove the three girls to Silver Shoe. She told them they had to be ready to leave by eight-fifteen, in order to get to school on time. She waited for them in the car, checking emails on her Blackberry.

"Right," said Cally bossily, as they walked through the gate. "This morning, Tilly, you can help us muck out – there's a not-so-glamorous side to keeping a pony that I think you need to know about." She smiled.

Tilly didn't mind at all. To her it was all part of the fun of being at the farm – and she knew how important it was for the horses to have food, clean water and fresh bedding. Thankfully she was prepared. She was wearing a pair of jeans and an old sweatshirt. Her uniform was folded neatly in her bag, away from the dust and dirt.

The girls greeted Rosie and led her outside, then they went into the stable.

86

"We have to do this every day," explained Mia. "We start by clearing out the muck."

She pointed towards a pile of manure, and nudged Cally towards it.

"You always make me do this bit," groaned Cally, attacking the manure with her special shavings fork. "You're such a wimp, Mia!"

Mia giggled.

"Next, we dig
out any wet bedding
and replace it if
necessary. Princess
Rosie likes her layer
of bedding to be
comfy and thick,

fluffed up like pillows for when she lies
down – of course!"

"I can do that," said Tilly helpfully,
picking up the fork.

"We're lucky. Shavings are much easier to
muck out than straw," said Cally. "Rosie is on
shavings because she has an allergy to straw.
The odd racehorses Angela has in go on
shredded newspaper, which
is completely dust free.
I'll go and get some
fresh water and hay.
Just watch out for the
mice!"

The idea of mice
didn't bother Tilly. She
loved all animals.

To Tilly's delight, the girls invited her back to Silver Shoe after school. Twice in one day! This time, she visited Magic Spirit. He was looking much healthier and most of his sores had cleared up. But to Tilly, he still seemed sad and lonely which, in turn, made her feel sad. She wondered why he refused to come out of his barn – especially when there were so many lovely horses around the farm for him to make friends with.

Meanwhile, Angela was in the yard, lugging bags of feed down from a lorry. Tilly offered to help.

"Hello you. What's up?" said Angela, immediately noticing Tilly's mood. "It's a wonderful warm evening, and you've got a glum face."

"I wish," said Tilly. "I *wish* that Magic
Spirit would come out of his barn. It must be so
lonely in there. All the others are going off and
having fun, and he's on his own in the dark."

"Mmm, he'll come out when he's ready, I'm sure, but maybe he feels safe in there. You've done a great job earning his trust, Tilly. Don't feel bad."

Tilly nodded.

"My dad," explained Angela, "has trained hundreds of horses. And he says the most important thing of all is not to rush anything."

"Act like you've got ten years with a horse and the job will take ten minutes. Act like you've got ten minutes and it will probably take ten years!" said a voice behind them.

It was Jack Fisher. He'd overheard them talking. "It's an old cowboy saying," he said. "And a true one. That little fella, Magic Spirit, needs lots of patience and love. We don't know anything about what he's been through or what frightens him. It takes time to understand an animal who's been neglected, or through some kind of trauma."

"Maybe he's ready for you to groom him," said Angela to Tilly. "His coat really

needs some attention and I'm sure he'd like *you* to do it more than anyone else."

"Can I really?" said Tilly.

"I think it would be a good thing for both of you. I'll ask Duncan to give you some help, until Magic Spirit gets used to it all."

Tilly met Duncan in the clubroom, and she remembered what Mia had said about Cally fancying him. He *was* quite good-looking, with messy hair and twinkling blue eyes. He was suntanned from being outside a lot. But too old for Cally, thought Tilly – although maybe he and Angela would make a nice couple.

As they fetched a grooming kit from the tack room, Duncan explained how Angela had kindly given him the job of head boy when he had no money.

"I used to groom horses for the kids at Cavendish Hall – and then Jack Fisher spotted me at a local show. He said I had the makings of a top jockey. He introduced me to the lovely Angela, and the rest is history. I'm going to win big for the Fishers one day. You watch."

As soon as Tilly popped her head over Magic's door, he stepped forward and wickered softly. Duncan explained to Tilly that this was a sign of recognition, like mares and their foals make to each other.

Tilly was overjoyed. Quietly, she stepped into his box, taking her time, reassuring Magic that everything was fine. But as soon as Duncan followed her, Magic snorted, and straightaway became restless. So Duncan went back to the door, fascinated by what he saw.

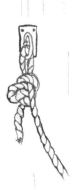

Tilly gently scratched Magic's favourite spot at the base of his neck, by his withers, and as he lowered his head, she gave him a carrot. Very slowly, she was able to put the head collar on him, but she didn't tie him up because she knew he would feel constrained. She just looped the rope through the ring next to his manger.

Starting at the base of his neck, she used the soft body brush on his thin coat. Gradually, much to Duncan's amazement, Magic started to relax, and enjoy this whole new experience of pampering. All the time, Tilly was chatting away to Magic, telling him about her dream of one day becoming a famous show jumper.

"Here," said Duncan, passing her a comb. "See if you can tidy up his mane and tail, but go carefully, because it looks as though there are a few knots in there."

As soon as Tilly tried to touch his mane,

Magic got anxious and immediately tossed his head so that Tilly could no longer reach. She moved onto his tail instead.

Tilly began to work the comb through Magic Spirit's tail, and as she did so, several long hairs came loose. She gathered them up and wound them around her wrist next to her bracelet.

"That's an unusual piece of jewellery," said Duncan, staring at her horsehair bracelet. "And yet, it's strangely familiar. I think I've seen one like it somewhere before . . . can't quite remember. Where did you get it?"

Tilly shrugged, because the truth was, she didn't know. The Redbrows had told her she was wearing the bracelet when they adopted her, looped three times around her wrist because she was so little. Now it was only looped twice, because she had grown.

95

As she finished polishing his coat with a stable rubber, Tilly asked Duncan, "Do you think Magic Spirit will ever want to go outside?"

"Why don't you ask him?" answered Duncan.

So Tilly leaned towards Magic Spirit's ear and asked, and at the same time she pointed towards the open door. Magic Spirit stepped back and began swishing his tail. Tilly knew this meant he was unhappy.

"There's your answer," said Duncan. "Something out there is bothering him – and I think I might know what it is."

Carefully he inspected Magic Spirit's coat, all the time soothing him with his voice.

"Look here," he showed Tilly, lifting Magic Spirit's mane. "Bite marks."

Tilly could see several raised scars, in the shape of teeth.

"Ow . . . that's awful! *Who* would do a thing like that?" she gasped, upset at the thought.

"Not *who*, but *what*. They're not human

bites. It looks to me like the work of another horse. It happens occasionally, I'm afraid. Some horses just don't get along with each other. When they're out in the field they push each other about. Maybe that explains why his owner abandoned him."

"Poor Magic Spirit," said Tilly sniffing as she stroked his forehead. Magic leaned across and rested his nose on her shoulder affectionately.

"It also explains," said Duncan, scratching his head, "why Magic Spirit is wary of going outside – the other horses might be a bother to him. He's probably frightened of being bitten again."

Tilly sighed.

"Don't worry," said Duncan. "We'll work on it. And at least we've learned a bit more about Magic Spirit's background now – I think we'll have to be extra sensitive when grooming his mane and face."

"It's a good job you noticed the marks," said Tilly.

"Well, it's thanks to you that I was able to. Without your help, I wouldn't have been able to get close enough to check. You're the only person who's been able to calm him."

Nine

At last the weekend arrived. Tilly had lost count of how many times she had thought about Magic Spirit and what he was doing. She couldn't wait to see him again. So much had happened. Two weeks ago she was admiring pictures of ponies in magazines. Now she was helping to look after real ones.

On Saturday, Tilly was desperate to go to Silver Shoe Farm, but Mr Redbrow insisted she tidied her bedroom and finished her homework first. This took all morning, and

her little brother, Adam, did everything he could to get in the way. While she was hoovering the carpet he kept pulling out the plug. When she was trying to concentrate on her English essay, he turned the television up as loud as he could.

"You little freak!" yelled Tilly. "Go and annoy someone else!"

Adam grinned and chased Scruff into the garden.

Tilly stared at the pile of schoolbooks in front of her and felt miserable. It was a perfect day for being outside with the horses – brilliant sunshine and blue skies – she could see it through the window, but she was stuck indoors working. A text from Cally only made her feel more frustrated:

R U COMING 2 FARM 2DAY? ME' N' MIA R GOING HACKING. X

She looked at her watch and replied:

MAYBE LATER. HOMEWORK FIRST (GROAN). X

Tilly carried on writing her essay, and as she did, she twiddled with her black horsehair bracelet. She'd put Magic's tail hairs in the special little box she kept on her dressing table. Her thoughts drifted to the idea of him, leaping fences, with her in the saddle. She imagined taking him to an event, maybe even Badminton – going cross-country and winning. She could hear the

commentator's voice: *Tilly Redbrow and Magic Spirit take the lead! Who'd have thought this shy rescue horse would have come as far as he has! What a performance!*

She looked down at her essay and realised she'd written, 'William Shakespeare wrote lots of horses . . .'

Suddenly her phone buzzed again. It was an answer-phone message from Mia:

"Hi, Tilly, listen, you've got to get to
the farm as soon as you can . . .
my battery's about to go . . .
something's happened to Magic Spirit . . .
you need to—"

The line went dead. Tilly felt her heart skip. She tried calling Mia back, but there was no connection. What had happened to Magic Spirit? Had there been an accident? Had he fallen ill?

There was only one way to find out. In a panic, she ran into the garden, where her dad was digging his vegetable patch and her mum was sweeping the path.

"Can I go to the farm? I've got to go to the farm! Can I? *Please!*" she begged, without stopping for breath.

Her parents looked up.

"What's all the fuss about, Tiger Lil'?" said her dad.

"Magic Spirit! Something's happened –
I need to see him!"

"But have you finished your homework?"
her dad said, using his sensible teacher's voice.

"Um . . . sort of . . . nearly," said Tilly,
flustered.

"I said chores and homework first," he
replied, shaking his head. "Come on, it won't
take you long. Magic Spirit can wait till
you've done that."

"But it might be too *late* by then," cried
Tilly. Adam stood behind her pulling faces.
"*Please!*" she begged. "Something's
happened."

"Maybe," said her mum, seeing how
desperate her daughter was. "Maybe I could
give you a lift when I drop Adam at football
practice – we'll be leaving in ten minutes."

Tilly clapped her hands together and
nodded hopefully.

"But what about your homework?"
muttered Mr Redbrow, scratching his head.

"She'll finish it tomorrow, won't you,
Tilly?"

Tilly and her mum winked at each other. Sometimes mums were the best thing in the world.

It took twenty minutes to drop Adam at his football club and then get to Silver Shoe Farm. Tilly fidgeted in her seat, full of nerves, as they drove through the tunnel of trees.

Mrs Redbrow pulled up and Tilly jumped out. She ran up the lane, and through the gate. Without noticing anything that was

going on in the yard, she went straight to Magic Spirit's barn. He wasn't there!

"Oh no," gasped Tilly. "I'm too late!"

Her eyes started to brim with tears and her hands trembled.

"Hello, Tilly," said a voice behind her. It was Duncan. "Too late for what?"

"Where's Magic Spirit? What's happened?" said Tilly, almost sobbing.

Duncan looked her and smiled.

"You look so worried, Tilly. You'd better come with me," he said, wrapping his arm around her shoulders.

As they walked, Tilly explained:

"I got this answer-phone message from Mia, but she got cut off . . . all it said was that I had to come to the farm, because something has happened to—"

They stopped at a small post and railed paddock behind the stables.

"She's right," nodded Duncan. "Something *has* happened. Look."

And there was Magic Spirit. He was standing outside in the sun, looking relaxed

106

and happy. Next to him was a skewbald
miniature pony, only half the size of Magic
Spirit!

"What a lovely sight, eh?"
said Duncan. "Come and
meet Thumbelina – Lina,
for short. I borrowed her
from a local farmer. I
thought she would have a
good effect on Magic Spirit,
and sure enough, they're
getting on brilliantly."

"But I thought . . . oh . . .
I was worried something
terrible had happened!"

Tilly realised she'd panicked for no
reason. Then she saw Mia walking across the
stable yard, smiling and waving.

"Hi, Tilly. You got my message then? I
was worried it wouldn't reach you. Great
news, isn't it?"

Tilly nodded.

"I thought you were trying to tell me
something awful had happened!"

107

"Sorry," said Mia. "I didn't mean to scare you. I just knew you'd want to see this."

"It's a trick I've used before," explained Duncan, as the girls looked on. "With another rescue horse. Little Lina is so good-natured, and because she's small she isn't a threat. Magic Spirit took to her straightaway. He's made a friend. Hopefully, she'll help him get his confidence back. And who knows? Maybe one day he'll be out grazing with the rest of gang. It's thanks to you, Tilly – you've been so patient with him."

Tilly watched as Magic Spirit sniffed Lina's ears. He seemed happier than ever before. Just then Angela came out of one of the stables. She joined them.

"Excellent," she said. "Duncan always has good ideas about how to settle the horses in. But we

couldn't have done it without you, Tilly –
well done. I think Magic Spirit and Lina are
going to make a great team."

"Even if they do look a bit mismatched,"
said Duncan. "Like a comedy double-act!"

Duncan and Angela laughed, but Tilly
simply stood back and smiled.

She was so proud of Magic Spirit. For a
moment he looked up and met her eye, then
carried on grazing. And Tilly knew in her
heart that this was going to be the start of
great things for him.

Pippa's Top Tips

With good training and positive experiences a horse will develop trust in humans. To build this trust, we need to respond calmly and consistently to their behaviour.

Although horses don't use words, their behaviour can reveal how they feel. Understanding horse behaviour is really important. For example, if a horse swishes its tail or pricks its ears back, it may be afraid. If a horse wickers at you, it's a sign of recognition. Mares make this gentle sound to their foals.

A good way to learn more about horses, whether you own one or not, is to spend time helping out at your local stables or riding school. The Pony Club is also a good starting point. Go to **www.pcuk.org** for more information.

Never be afraid to seek advice from people who have more experience with horses than you.

Owning a horse requires continuous care and commitment. Make sure you can give enough time before you consider this option. You may be able to share the responsibilities with a friend.

Always be aware of the horse's hind legs. Even the quietest horse will kick out at a fly, and if you're in the wrong place at the wrong time, you'll get hurt.

Always check your horse's legs for cuts or swellings before you get on to ride. If you don't, you could cause more damage, or even lameness.

A set of horse shoes normally last around five to six weeks. Most good stables will keep a notebook listing all the dates of when the horses were last shod.

Make sure your horse is safely tied, but use a quick-release, or slip-knot. Some horses don't like the idea of being constrained and it makes them panic.

There are lots of different brushes for grooming horses: a Dandy brush is stiff-bristled, used to loosen dirt – work it in circular motions across the body, but be gentle around the thinner-skinned areas; a stable rubber is a soft rag used to remove any remaining dirt – it makes the horse's coat lovely and shiny; finally, use a comb and conditioning spray to work through the mane and tail.

Acknowledgements

Three years ago when my autobiography was published
I never imagined that I would find myself writing
children's books. Huge thanks go to Louisa Leaman
for helping me to bring Tilly to life, and to
Jennifer Miles for her wonderful illustrations.

Many thanks to Fiona Kennedy for persuading and
encouraging me to search my imagination and for all her
hard work, along with the rest of the team at Orion.
Due to my riding commitments I am not the easiest
person to get hold of as my agent Jonathan Marks
at MTC has found. It's a relief he has been able
to work on all the agreements for me.

Much of my thinking about Tilly has been done
out loud in front of family, friends and godchildren –
thank you all for listening.

More than anything I have to acknowledge my four-legged
friends – my horses. It is thanks to them, and the
great moments I have had with them, that I was able to
create a girl, Tilly, who like me follows her passions.

Pippa Funnell
Forest Green, February 2009